The 'G
House

A. L. MOTTLEY

ISBN-10: 1976181968
ISBN-13: 978-1976181962

DEDICATION

I dedicate this book to you, the reader because it's you who I write for.

I hope I make you cry a little and laugh a lot.

And also, to the memory of my Nana Flo and her best friend Alice, whose conversations at the kitchen table were unintentional comedy gold.

I was blessed to have you in my real world. I hope I've done you proud in the world I've created for you

Assumptions can cause murder!

PROLOGUE

"So what do you think Bob"?

"Well, you seem to have it all sorted luv"

Bob, back seated in his favourite chair, following the departure of their surprise visitors looked over at his wife, Flo, a tad taller than him, with a shapely hourglass figure, albeit hidden somewhat by her eternal pinny wearing, and a face more often than not with a smile on it. A face beautiful to him and pleasant at the least to others, brown eyes her brows naturally well shaped, a slim slightly hooked nose, above average sized lips, sometimes with a slick of red lipstick, sometimes not. Flo was never one for make-up, a fact that pleased him, some of 'em looked like clowns nowadays, not his Flo, straight reddish brown hair, shoulder length and tied back in a bun for practicality, framed the vision of loveliness before him. At night he got to see her hair, in all its beauty, as he watched her routine of a hundred brush strokes a night, her hair not yet greying and when released from its ribbon, would tumble down over her neck, sometimes falling over her face, as she bent, a la, Veronica Lake. Daft on the girls who tried wearing that style at work in the factories, during the war but, sensual on his darling Flo.
His own hair, a matter of pride too, long having lost its natural blonde hue, it was now completely grey but, he'd not lost a hair of it... In the end, he'd die with a full head

of hair, but, that was a long way off for now, regardless of the age gap.

Flo was thirty years his junior, they'd been the 'talk of the town' for a while, when their courtship had become public knowledge, mainly because of Flo's best friend, Alice, and her gob!

He'd first met Flo, following her move into next door, the local doctors surgery and home to the doctor and his young family, as a live in maid. By the time of their first encounter, he'd been a widower for almost five years, his first wife dying young from consumption. Having fought and served in the Great War, it could rightly be assumed that he'd be most likely to die first, instead he went to war a married man, and came home a widower.

His grief, at first seemed endless, but eventually the pain subsided and the good memories took their place. He was at this stage in his life when he first laid eyes on Flo, and he fell for her, hook line and sinker. The only thing making him hesitate was the difference in their ages but, unbeknownst to him at the time, Flo had experienced the same rush of emotions, and *she* didn't give two hoots about the age gap.

 The gossips had said it wouldn't last when they'd first married but, here they were more than fifteen years later, happy as the proverbial *Larry*, with a teenage daughter in tow and now an offer from out of the blue, that would benefit them financially. Bob did have a fair pension from his job as a clerk and he still worked part-time, helping out in a couple of local shops. On top of that, Flo was a grafter and had various cleaning jobs, they got by, but, any luxuries required sacrifice, so this job offer, although it meant Flo working and sleeping away for a month, would mean they could afford one of those twin tubs she was always going on about and have more than enough left over to add to their nest egg fund. *"It'll come in handy when our Joyce gets wed"* Flo had said, when weighing up the pros and cons of the offer.

Now aged fifteen and working like many others in Moston, at Ferrantis factory, Joyce was walking out with Lawrence, a lad she'd gone to school with, and it was long accepted by both families that eventually they'd get married. This plan met with Bob's approval but,Flo wasn't so sure. She thought back to Lawrence's many visits for 'tea'

'I've never known anyone so young, be so old headed, and boring'

She knew it wouldn't last, she'd often seen Joyce's eyes glaze over when he was talking. Joyce wanted more, she wanted glamour, she wanted tall dark and handsome, like her favourite leading man, Victor Mature and even though she'd be mortified at the thought of ever discussing romance with a parent, she knew her mum understood, especially when she turned round from peeling spuds one day, to see Joyce staring into space, and said,

3

"You'll know the one when he comes along luv, just like I did the first day I met your dad...Now, if you've nowt better to do than stare into space, you can cut these into chips"

Joyce most definitely knew that Lawrence wasn't the 'one' but, said nothing and hurriedly started chipping the spuds, hoping to spare the embarrassment of having to listen to old people talk about love.

Bob's voice interrupted Flo's thoughts "sorry luv" she said "I was miles away, say that again?"

"I was just saying, it's up to you Flo, you're the one who'll be doing it"

"I want to but I don't" replied Flo, still very unsure "I've never spent so long away from you before and what about our Joyce?"

"Our Joyce is fifteen, not five, she's already a working girl, she can do my tea and we'll both keep up with the housework, so don't fret that you'll be coming back to a hovel, I kept this place spick and span when I lived here alone remember?"

"You did that" Flo agreed "But you didn't have your leg then"

Bob burst into raucous laughter "Of course I had my leg you daft sausage., the doctor said I'd have problems as I got older, but mostly in winter, its July now, and you'll only be gone for four weeks, I can't see it getting cold enough for snow, during that time" he paused and put his arms around his wife "If you want to go, you have my blessing" Flo, hugged him, before stepping back and saying "I need a brew and a cig, it's a lot to take in is this"

"Well, you sit down luv, and I'll bring you a cuppa, and then I need to pop outside and I may be some time" he winked at her and went to get the tea, as he smiled at his favourite way of saying he was going to the toilet "you have a good think luv" he said, returning with a brew "you don't want the paper do you? I was gonna take it with me" "No luv" said Flo taking the cup of tea from him.

As Bob went on his half hour visit to the outside loo, Flo lit a cigarette, sat back, and recalled the surprising events of earlier on..

***

Between the witching hour and the darkest part of the night, when silence reigned over the suburbs, was her time, the chance to be alone, and have much needed respite from the demands of the day... The demands of him. but, he could wait for a few hours, this was her time. She straightened her skirt and sat at the dressing table, an array of make up carefully lined up on a white handkerchief. Neatness was of the utmost importance to her, a place for everything and for everything a place, meant nothing went missing, and nothing got found out of place.

Looking carefully at her reflection, she felt a little embarrassed at her pleasure in the reflection before her, but, she was good at what she did, and she dismissed 'false modesty' with a kiss blown to the mirror. She'd perfected the art of subtlety in her make up, in another life she'd have been a make up artist in Hollywood, she was convinced that if Bette Davis didn't wear her foundation so thick she'd look years younger, and prettier.

Well groomed eyebrows, perfectly arched and highlighted with a mid brown pencil, subtle but effective, framing smoky blue eyes, their upper and lower lids edged in immaculately winged black eyeliner and black mascara, a subtle glow of rouge to her cheeks and lipstick a pinky red tone, inexplicably labeled 'Summer breeze' completed her look. She ran her finger through her blonde hair, shoulder length and wavy, just brushing the straps of her gown. She liked this look.

Suddenly the thought came,

'But, what about him? He hates to see me like this. He wants me bowed and dowdy, he wants me hidden. We can't go on like this...I'm at breaking point'

She looked in the mirror, the carefully applied wings now traveling down her cheeks, carried by the wave of tears and the anger. He'd promised she wouldn't be locked away anymore, he'd promised to trust her and let her have a little freedom, no one around here barely knew him, that's why they'd moved here. No one would judge how he was with her, no 'tuts' or disgusted looks, but, he'd lied yet again. This was the sixth time they'd moved in as many years. and nothing had changed. He only spoke to her when they were alone. sometimes he ignored her for days, and the feelings of mind numbing loneliness, were starting to come back. It was the same everywhere they went, the promises that always came to nothing.

"I won't hide you, it'll be different here...I know I said that last time, but bear with me"

She'd sighed and said nothing, it'd been this way for an eternity, but, what could she do. She needed him as much as he needed her. He'd never let her go, she'd never leave him. The only means of escape she could see, after so many years under his control, was death.

A thought came in her head, she tried to ignore it and opened a jar of cold cream and began removing her make up, then she changed into her nightclothes, the thought was still there, she yawned as if the yawn would push the thought away, it seemed to work. She climbed into bed, tiredness suddenly overwhelming her, 'a few hours rest til he needs me' she thought, her body wriggling in an attempt to get comfy. She closed her eyes, willing sleep to come before the thought came back.

The thought won.

'If one of us has to die, why should it be me?'

CHAPTER 1

Flo had just finished tidying up after breakfast, when she heard the knock on the door, it was a Saturday, so breakfast had been a relaxed affair, the full works for her and Bob, bacon, sausage, egg, *runny for her, hard for Bob,* with bread, fresh from the bakery, slathered in 'best butter' their teenage daughter Joyce, settling for toast and jam, and Flo practically had to force that down her. Apparently she was dieting. "*There's nowt on ya"* Flo had retorted, when her only child had refused anything more. She wouldn't have even eaten that if there hadn't been an accompanying threat from her Mam. *"No breakfast, no trip to town with your mates"* Dad, as usual said nowt, he just wanted a quiet life.

She'd recently noticed that her her Dad was older than her friend's Dads. It didn't really bother her, he was a lovely Dad, but she wished he was a bit more 'with it' they might have a record player if he was. The new Frankie Vaughan single had just been released and she was desperate to listen to it in the record shop, they only had a radiogram at home, so she'd stuffed a piece of toast down and scarpered off, the warning ringing in her ears,

"Make sure you're home for tea. It's not the Midland Hotel, there won't be a second sitting"

"I wonder who that can be?" Flo said, as the door knocked a second time "it'll probably be your shadow" said Bob, referring to her best mate "when does Alice ever knock?" queried Flo with raised eyebrows, she knows the door's unlocked all day, and anyway, she's gone on a day trip to Marple, with Joan from next door to her"

"Joan, who she can't stand?" asked Bob with a shake of his head "the one she's forever calling when she comes round here?"

"Well, Joan's other mate took ill. I think she had a stroke, and not even forty yet, so the ticket was free" The door knocked again, "I'd better see who it is" and she headed to the front door, Bob said no more, Alice was well known for her love of anything free. *She'd go to Blackpool with Hitler, if he was paying*, he thought, and went back to reading his newspaper.

"Hold your horses, I'm coming" shouted Flo as the door knocked yet again, just before she went to open it. And when she did, she nearly fell down in shock, there, stood large as life, at the front door, were her former employers Doctor and Mrs Howarth! both as slim as she remembered them, if a tad older now, and still impeccably dressed. Mrs Howarth's heels, making her seem taller than her husband at his five feet eight inches, but eye to eye with Flo, who although in her tartan slippers, had the advantage of standing on her front door step.

"Hello Florence" said Doctor Howarth gaily, when there was no reply Mrs Howarth added "Hello dear"

Flo stood open mouthed for a few more seconds before speaking "Bloomin' eck., oh my! I've not seen you two since God knows when!"

"Six months after you got married" replied Mrs Howarth she paused before asking "erm *how* is Bob? is he still -
"Alive?" Interjected Flo, "Yeah he's in the back room"
There was no malice in her answer, when you married a much older man, it was a question often asked and it *had* been over almost fifteen years since last they'd seen each other. "Gordon Bennet! where are my manners" said Flo, realising they were all still stood at the front door. come in, come in. I can't believe you've caught me in me pinny"

"Florence!" teased the doctor "You're *always* in your pinny"

Flo laughed as she welcomed them into the lobby, before leading them towards the back room, forewarning Bob by shouting "BOB, WE'VE GOT VISITORS" Bob hurriedly put his jacket on, sleeves still rolled up, and stood with pipe in mouth, waiting to see who it was. He was as surprised as his wife had been. "Well I never! How do, Doctor Howarth, Mrs Howarth, long time no see"

Not much younger than Bob, the doctor had known him as patient and neighbour for over a decade before Flo had come to live and work at the surgery. While Bob and the visitors greeted each other and reminisced, Flo conjured up a pot of tea, some Madeira cake and custard cream biscuits, and invited all to sit at the table, as she 'poured', the doctor cleared his throat and said. "Well, I suppose you'll both wondering why we're here?" Flo as usual replied for the two of them. "It had crossed me mind eh, it's not your Philip is it?" she asked with concern in her voice, for their only child "Oh no nothing like that, smiled the doctor, knowing Flo's genuine love for their son. "Philip is fine and dandy. Not married yet, before you ask" he said with a wink "but, he's a great help in the running of the guest house. He's our accountant and helps out a lot with the day to day things"

"I was about to ask that next" said Flo referring to 'Oakenelm', the guest house her former employers had bought following the doctor's retirement "so you've still got it? How *is* business?"

"Well, that's the reason we're here Flo, we're in a bit of a pickle and you might be able to help us out?"

"Flo took a deep breath, and spoke at machine gun speed "I'd walk on hot coals for you two, you've always been nothing but kindness itself to me and Bob, but, if it's about working at the guest house, well, I've just got too much on and you're two buses away, you know I like to stay local"

"Calm down Florence" said the doctor, putting his hand on hers, and hear me out, before you say anything else"

"Okay" she replied hesitantly.

"We *would* like you to run the guest house, but, only on a temporary basis, you wouldn't need to get any buses, because we'd be asking you to live in for four weeks and four weeks *only"* He paused a moment "And you'd be paid this much for your service" He handed a piece of paper with a figure written on it, to Flo, she glanced at it and gulped. "*How much* ?" she said almost spitting out her tea. She passed the paper to Bob who stopped puffing his pipe, immediately, a *more* than generous amount was being offered. "Let me explain" said the doctor, he glanced at his wife, who gave his hand a supportive squeeze, and he began to speak.

"As you know Flo, we took on the guest house as an investment when I retired, we would have loved you to have taken up our offer of the housekeeper's job but, we understood, with you being a newlywed and everything else, and having commitments" he paused for a sip of tea "and as luck would have it, we were blessed to find another housekeeper just as good as you"

"Not quite as good, darling" interrupted his wife, with a wink unseen by Flo, "no one will ever be as good a housekeeper as Flo"

"I stand corrected my dear"

Flo gave a satisfied sigh, and the doctor continued

"It's long been a dream of ours to go on a Mediterranean

cruise, we're not getting any younger and this year decided to take the plunge. The guest house has been a terrific success, so we can more than afford it and thus, we find ourselves due to set off from Southampton docks in less than two weeks"

"Sounds wonderful" said Flo still confused as to why they were here. if the guest house was a success and the housekeeper excellent, what did they want from her?

"Well it *was* all wonderful" sighed Mrs Howarth "until disaster struck"

"Has the boat sunk?"

"No" she smiled, "both our housekeeper and her husband got hit by a bus and are in hospital with broken legs, and a fracture or two, as we speak"

"They both got hit by buses on the same day?" asked Flo in amazement. "what an awful coincidence"

"Not exactly" replied Mrs Howarth, stifling another smile. "they got hit by the *same* bus"

Flo stifled an urge to laugh "How did that happen?"

"Well, according to Mrs Basker -that's our housekeeper, they'd just come out of the Gaumont, after seeing a George Formby film, and were headed to the bus stop. It was a bit of a foggy night and drizzly, They saw their bus pulling away and realising they'd have a bit of a wait, started to cross the road at a more leisurely pace, however unbeknowst to the both of them, another bus had pulled up at the same time"

"I hate it when that happens. The eighty-eight's a buggar for it -scuse me language- you wait ages and two turn up at once"

"Anyway" continued the doctor's wife after nodding in agreement with Flo's complaint. *not that it bothered her, she never went on buses.* "that was the *one* that hit them"

"Oh!"

"And they'll be in hospital for at least another four to six weeks"

"Ah! during the time you'll be on the cruise" said Flo, starting to understand the reason for their visit "but why would you need me? how I can help? won't your Philip be here whilst you're away? you've already said he does a good job"

"Yes, he certainly does" agreed Mrs Howarth, "and he can work at the guest house weekends, but, as luck would have it, or bad luck it seems, our time away on the cruise is when we're having some modernisations done on the house. We're not getting any younger and Doctor Howarth is suffering with leg aches" She paused and looked at her husband, he motioned for her to continue "So we're having a downstairs bedroom added, and need Philip to be at the house during the week, to supervise the builders. If it wasn't for the building work, we'd get agency staff and leave Philip in charge, but this building work is much needed, hence our dilemma, and consequent visit to you"

Flo said nothing, and Mrs Howarth continued " The place practically runs itself, the staff are excellent, you won't be on your own, and the sum mentioned covers the cost of someone of your own choosing, coming with you to help" Still no response from Flo, so she continued "Philip would be there *every* weekend, and just at the end of the phone during the week. You'll have your own quarters" She searched her mind for other enticements. "There'll be lists of everything you need to know, oh please say yes Florence?"

"I'm all of a fluster, I don't know what to say. what do you think Bob?" she turned to her husband with questioning eyes,

"It's up to you lass"

Thanks, she thought, *you're no bloody help at all.* "Let me clear these pots away, I can't think in mess"

"I'll help you" said Mrs Howarth, and ignoring Flo's refusal of assistance, she picked up a couple of plates, and pushed the scullery door closed as she followed her in to the kitchen.

"Flo" she whispered "between you and me there's something you need to know, Hugh's not well, and he's not going to get any better. He doesn't think I know, but you don't get to be a doctors wife for this long without knowing the signs, this is going to be his last holiday. I'm sorry to tell you like this, and I'm sorry if it seems like I'm trying to make you feel obliged, but, I need to do this for him" Her eyes filled with tears, Flo handed her a hanky from her pinny pocket "It's clean, wipe your eyes and go and sit down luv, I'll be in in a minute" She gently pushed her towards the door, as she closed it behind her, Flo began to sob quietly, and as her tears fell, she thought, and came to a decision.

"I'll do it" she said walking back in from the scullery, the relief on the faces of her visitors was tangible, Bob merely looked at her and puffed his pipe. "and I've got a good idea for someone to do it with me" she continued

"Oh Flo, we're forever in your debt" responded Mrs Howarth.

"Well, I'm saying I'll do it, but don't get your hopes up too much, I need to check with someone first"

"Of course" said the pair, eager to please, and get a definite answer.

"You remember Alice don't you?" said Flo

"Is she still alive? she was always at deaths door" chuckled the doctor, before adding "you didn't hear me say that"

"Yes she's still alive" said Flo with a grin "still dying, but, slowly" she was glad of the humour in the room, after Mrs Howarth's revelation, she now realised how weary the doctor looked "It's all a bit of a rush is this, but I'll pop round and see her later and if you can get back to me?"

"We can come round tomorrow if you like?" replied the doctor

"Gosh it is a rush innit? okay, leave it with me and I'll see what I can do, no promises, you know Alice, she can turn on a penny, but, I'll do me best" remembering the doctor's condition, she added "If needs be I'll come on me own, I'm sure me and your Philip can manage between us"

The wave of relief that washed over the doctor and his wife was evident in their beaming smiles..

"Well, we'll take our leave and let you get on with what you need to do, we can call round tomorrow afternoon around four if that's okay with you?" Said the doctor, not waiting for an answer as he put on his coat and shook Bob's hand. Flo replied "four o clock will be fine" as she led them to the door.

"You're a lifesaver Flo" whispered Mrs Howarth, as she waited for her husband to open the car door for her"

"I wish" she replied poignantly, and then she hugged the doctor's wife, gave him a wave and watched til the car could no longer be seen.

She went inside, drank tea and mulled everything over in her mind, whilst Bob sat on the toilet, mulling over which horse to back in the two-thirty.

"So it's settled then?" he queried upon his return, having decided to back a horse called 'Surprise Visit'

"It is if I can get Alice to come"

"Why her though? what about Brenda?"

"Which Brenda?"

"The one who used to mind our Joyce, she's in her twenties now and she can get the time off cos she works in her dads shop. Between you and me, he could do with a break from her he was telling me the other day that he wished she'd get bloody wed, and move out"

"No, I'm taking Alice, firstly Dr Howarth knows her well, and whatever she is, she's as honest as the day is long, and spotless. And if I don't take her, she'll drive you mad coming round every day to ask if you've heard from me, and you know I'm not lying"

"You're not wrong"sighed Bob realising the truth of what she'd said "yeah, take her with you!"

"I'd better nip round now and tell her all about it.Give us a kiss, I'll be back in time to do the tea, and keep me fingers crossed whilst you do the pools" Bob did as he was told, planting an affectionate kiss on her cheek.. She shoved her coat on, dashed out of the door, and practically skipped round to to her friend's. She loved her life, loved her husband and daughter, but, she said to herself, *I'm entitled to a bit of a change. Entitled to a bit of excitement and new surroundings.* If Alice agreed, and she wouldn't leave her house til she did, it'd be a good 'change' for them. It'd all come a surprise, she'd normally be on Conran street Market of a Saturday. She was looking forward to the 'adventure' to come, a change was as good as a rest. And what an adventure it would turn out to be.

CHAPTER 2

Bang, bang! Flo knocked on the door, knowing Alice would be back from her day trip but, never left her door unlocked. She knocked again, this time louder.

"What brings you here?" said Alice in surprise as she answered the door "why aren't you on the market"

"I don't bloody work on it" came the curt reply "You'd think you did" replied her friend.

Dressed as usual in one of her favoured twinsets with sensible skirt, Alice was a couple of inches shorter than Flo, at around five foot three inches, but, of a similar build, she more often than not *seemed* the same height, her penchant for heels an antidote to Flo comfy shoes.

"You're lucky you caught me, I've only been back five minutes. Never again! that Joan is a right cow, and why were you banging like the rent man?" she said, suddenly realising that Flos, visit was 'out of the norm' she was somewhat petulant as she let her friend in, unlike Flo, her door was locked when she was home, and she wasn't pleased about having to answer it. She didn't like people the same way Flo did and she hated it when people just barged in your house, which *was* the norm round here. Having said that, she knew her friend would have a good reason for her visit, and being naturally inquisitive she wanted to know what it was.

Her and Flo were opposites in many ways, her hair blonde and curly, Flo's brown and straight. Flo happily married, Alice a bitter widow, cheated on and abandoned by her husband of a few months. The silver lining in the cloud of her marriage being the fact he was killed in a tragic accident a few weeks after leaving her, and as they were still legally married, she got the insurance payout and a tidy little pension for life. She knew she could afford to move into a semi in Alkrington if she wanted to, but she'd lived round here all her life and there were more people to look down on here, on her street of terraced houses. None of 'em were nicer than hers, she even had stone lions either side of her back gate.

Flo walked past her, down the lobby or corridor as Alice pretentiously called it, she liked pretension did Alice, although she referred to it as refinement and taste, Flo called it being a snob,

"Let me get me coat off first and put the kettle on, I can't stop long, I've got to put the tea on, mind you" she said, looking at the time on Alice's cuckoo clock, "at this rate we'll be having tea at supper time"

"You should get your Joyce doing it more often" said Alice with a sniff "you do her no favours mollycoddling her"

"And how did you become such an expert on kids?

considering you've got none of your own?" spat back Flo "and anyway, she's minding Mrs Baker's kids so shut it" She hated anyone talking about her Joyce, especially in that tone, Alice said nothing in return and went down the small step to her scullery where Flo heard the kettle being filled, she took off her coat and hung it on the hook behind the door, then, she looked around for an ashtray, and found one on the sideboard. Alice smoked but, not as much as Flo, in fact, Flo only knew one person who didn't smoke -Jan, from Edward street, she'd had to flick her ash in her handbag, when she'd popped round to hers for a brew, and the cheeky cow had opened the sash window, in the middle of winter an' all , no such problem here. Alice, though barely a smoker in Flo's eyes, she could make a packet of twenty last a week!, had loads of ashtrays.

Flo sat at the table and lit a cigarette, after a few moments she shouted to Alice,

"Have you gone to China for that tea?"

Alice returned with a tray and set it on the table "Do you want tea or dishwater, I was letting it mash whilst I wiped the sink. Anyway, *what* brings you round here?"

"I've got summat to tell you"

"If it's about Doreen Michaels, I already know... The tart!"

"Well I don't" said Flo with raised eyebrows, forgetting

for a moment why she was there, Alice began to tell her the juicy gossip but Flo interrupted her. "Tell me another time this is more important"

"More important than the shame of being caught with your knickers down, up an entry?"

"Ooh the tart! But, yeah it is. Listen to this, and let me get to the end before you say a word. And I mean it!"

Alice, eager to know what was going on, made a 'my lips are sealed' gesture with her finger to her mouth, and sat with increasing wonderment as Flo told her all about the doctor and his wife's visit and request for help. When she'd finished she lit a cigarette took a drag and said

"So what do you think? you'd be doing me a massive favour, I could finally afford twin tub, and if truth be told I've always fancied running a guest house. It's long been a dream of mine. Who knows ,we might sell our house and get a little guest house of our own when we both retire"

"Bob already has!" replied her friend sarcastically

"He's still got his bookies job"

"The only way your Bob is coming out of that house is feet first"

"Do you mind!" said Flo with an air of indignation. "that's my husband you're wishing into an early grave" Alice grimaced "You know what I mean, his first wife's parents bought that house from brand new and it was only a year or two before they drowned on the Titanic and Bob's Missus got left the house. Bob'll never move"

"Well, I'm Bob's missus now" Said Flo, huffily " And they did *not* drown on the Titanic they drowned in the Canal! She fell in, he jumped after her, and her petticoats dragged em both down. Bob's told me all about it" She saw the smirk on her friend's face and knew she was being 'wound up' She tutted, then sighed and took a sip of her tea.

"So, how much are they willing to pay?" asked Alice, still smiling at her 'Titanic' quip, Flo showed her the paper Doctor Howarth had written on "your share's in that too"

Alice, was visibly impressed by the sum offered "And how much would I get?"

Flo rooted briefly through her handbag and brought out a pen, she scribbled an amount on the paper and showed it to Alice. It was more than fair, but, then again the doctor and his missus sounded desperate. She looked at Flo before speaking, Alice could have a cutting tongue but she also had a kind heart where her best friend was concerned, she was more than aware that she was far more comfortable financially than her friend she was also aware that her friend was a proud woman, so, she picked her words carefully and craftily before replying.

"You know me Flo, I won't do owt for nowt, but, I won't

take owt for nowt either, and at the end of the day you're in charge, so, it dunt seem fair for me to take that amount, when you're gonna be doing most of the work. You know I have a weak chest and there's no way I'm doing toilets, so I'm happy to take this much" She wrote a revised amount on the paper

"Are you sure" said Flo? Quite taken aback but unsuspecting of her friend's real motives,

"I've said I'm not cleaning toilets, at this rate of pay I'm not gonna feel guilty about it"

"So, it that a yes to coming with me? I have to rush you cos they're coming back tomorrow, to see if we can do it or not"

"Looks like all their prayers have been answered" winked Alice "what time will they get to yours? I'll come round"

"About tea-time -which reminds me, I've got to get Bob's tea on and get the jelly going for tomorrows trifle"

"And you're sure Bob's alright with it"

"Hundred percent luv, I think he'll be glad of the peace especially if *you're* not coming round every day"

"Cheeky cow" she said, with affection, and stood up to see Flo to the door " I'll see you tomorow" she said before shutting the door. She was looking forward to the next few weeks. A change was as good as a rest.

The next morning Alice, as expected, turned up a good hour before she was supposed to. Bob having remembered an 'errand' he had to run, had gone out straight after Sunday dinner. Flo suspected the errand was a ruse to be out when Alice came, it *was* Sunday after all, where was open? He wasn't a church going man, he'd probably gone over to his sister's, and he'd taken Joyce with him so, that was a blessing, she couldn't cope with her teenage sighing as she flicked through her film magazines, and Joyce shared her dad's contempt for Alice. 'Nosy cow' being the thought that most ran through her head when in her company. It was best that they weren't there.

She tried to ignore Alice's constant questions, and concentrated on getting the tea ready, ham butties as usual but, she'd cut them into triangles for the the special visitors, and had removed the crusts,

"I don't know if they have a lift. We'll ask that when they get here"

"No, you won't be expected to clean all the toilets, we've already been through that!"

At four o clock on the dot the front door knocked, A relieved Flo said "I'll get it" as she pushed Alice aside, glad to get away from her for a second "you sit down, you're a bloody guest"

She showed the doctor and his wife into the room, made

the re-introductions and waited a while whilst Alice talked about things that nobody ever remembered the way she did

"Oh Mrs Howarth, my mam went to her grave, praising your whore's dovers"

"I beg your pardon!"

"I particularly enjoyed the crab ones in the little puff pastry shells. In fact I've still got the recipes you wrote down for her"

"Ah" said the doctor's wife realising Alice meant hor d'oeuvres, and thankfully nothing more was said as Flo interrupted Alice's trip down memory lane by plonking a plate of ham butties in front of her "Will you bring the trifle in please Alice it's on the windowsill in the front parlour"

"I though I was a guest"

Flo threw her a warning look and Alice trotted off to get the trifle.

"Sorry about that" she said quietly to her guests "she's not changed a bit" said the Doctor with a smile "Unfortunately not" replied Flo with a wink. On Alice's return, they all enjoyed a tasty Sunday tea, and with Bob and Joyce's share covered up and put away, got down to business.

"I've had a word with Alice, and she's happy to come

with me, aren't you Alice?" said Flo, and without waiting for a reply she added "You said summat about a list of what to do's?"

"Indeed" said the doctor with an air of relief, and Mrs Howarth pulled from her handbag, a large thick brown envelope "Everything you need to know, is written down here" she said, handing over the package to Flo. "the guest list, staff list and duties, contact numbers for tradesmen, and there's an envelope that contains travel expenses, we don't want you traveling by bus with all your luggage, I've enclosed enough for a taxi"

Flo pulled a face, Alice grinned in delight. "We know you Flo" said the doctor. "getting a taxi isn't a waste, it's practicality, you'll have luggage so promise us you'll get a taxi" A reluctant Flo said "I promise" she'd have been fine getting the bus, but, if they insisted... Knowing Flo always kept her word Alice was delighted.

After a quick look through the package with Mrs Howarth, and an offer from them to reverse the charges if she needed to speak to them about anything, prior to them leaving. Goodbyes and thank you's were said, then Flo saw off the doctor and his wife.

She returned to an excited Alice "A staff list Flo" she clapped her hands in delight "We have staff!" Flo rolled her eyes "I don't want to hear another word on the subject tonight, Bob and Joyce will be home soon, so we'll go through the package tomorrow. We've still got over a week before we go, come round to mine tomorrow and we'll go through everything"

It was a slightly disappointed Alice that left the house. she was dying to know what was in all the envelopes. Still, tomorrow wasn't far off, and she was an early riser. She deliberately ignored Flo's shout of "AND DON'T BE COMING ROUND AT THE CRACK OF DAWN" as she let herself out.

CHAPTER 3

As feared, Alice turned up whilst the Billy the milkman was still there. An old friend of Bob's he always popped in of a Monday morning for a cuppa and a chat. Flo looked livid as Alice walked in with a cheery "Hiya, I knew you'd be up" but she ignored Flo, and turned to Billy "My milk was on 'the turn' the day after you delivered it, last Wednesday"

"I'll knock it off your bill", he replied, too wise to argue with her. I'll be getting off Flo, tell your Bob I'll see him next week if I don't see him in the pub"

"I'll see you to the door Billy" replied Flo. At the door Billy lowered his voice "you've got the patience of a saint Flo"

"I have haven't I" she said with a smile "and don't forget you owe me a gold top. I told you she'd be round before you left"

When she returned to the living room,Alice was sitting on the settee trying to look casual. Flo knew she'd been ear-wigging at the living room door,

"I'm getting dead excited now Flo, only a few more days til we're running a guest house"

"*I'm* running a guest house" Flo corrected her. "you're

assisting me" she checked the teapot, there was enough for a couple more cups so, she sat down at the table and started to pour. "do you want one,?" she asked, without even looking at Alice

"When do I ever say no, replied Alice coming to join her. She shot a look at the package "aren't you gonna open that?"

"Yeah when you've gone" Flo laughed at the look of disappointment that suddenly appeared on Alice's face "Of course I'm gonna open it, you *daft* apeth. I want us knowing what we need to know, off by heart, by the time we get there, so concentrate and don't ask daft questions"

Alice decided to bite her tongue, there was plenty of time to be offended, right now she wanted to know what was in the package. Flo tipped it up and a series of manilla envelopes of varying sizes fell out. She picked up one of the smaller ones and read what was written on it, she broke out in a broad smile, put her hand to her chest and said "Aw, bless 'em"

"What does it say?" asked Alice excitedly. Flo continued clutching her chest "It says taxi fare, and underneath in Mrs Howarth's handwriting -thank God! or I wouldn't have been able to read it. the doctor's is summat shocking. A frustrated Alice interjected "So what does it say?"

Flo took her hand from her chest and read aloud, "*Flo, we insist you take a taxi. We know you'll be 'pulling a* *face' but, you'll have bags and the trip across town will be tiring. And this is also our way of thanking you for stepping into th*e *breech at such short notice.,* she read on some more "Then, she's written in capital letters, taxi, *not* bus"

"Aw, int that nice? I'm gonna need at least two suitcases for a month away. I was dreading having to get a bus" Flo looked at her, in disbelief "What the eck do you need two suitcases for? and have you even got two suitcases? I'm taking three outfits one on, one in the wash, and one spare, and me pinnys I'll get all mine in the one suitcase and that includes shoes. We won't be getting a day off remember, that's why we're getting so well paid and we have to do the cooking on Sundays cos the cook doesn't come in so, don't be planning on any day trips out and about"

"Well, I won't be lowering me standards for anyone" replied Alice in a haughty tone "and of course I've got two suitcase, *and* a hatbox to match, I got 'em from Kendals. I'm taking what I need and seeing as we're going in a taxi I don't know what you're moaning about!"

Flo, tutted "The taxi will be leaving from here so good luck getting your suitcases round, cos I won't be helping you!"

"*I'll make two trips*" Alice mumbled to herself. "What's in the other envelopes?"

"This one's a list of the staff working with us"

"Don't you mean, *for* us?"

"God give me strength! don't be coming over all high and mighty madam" threatened Flo, before turning her attention to the other envelopes. "Aw bless her. Mrs Howarth's written down their working hours, duties and a little bit about them" She read on for a few moments, in silence "Apparently Liz the chambermaid is a right whizz at bed making" She said, picking up another envelope to open. "This one's the staff rota for the weeks we'll be there, this one's got a room plan in it, I'll get Bob to explain that one to me, and this big un is a day to day guide for me and you. This is the one we'll concentrate on"

"Can I have another brew first? this one tastes stewed"

"You still drank it though, dint ya? you make it then" Alice tutted and went to put the kettle on, whilst she was preparing the tea, Flo read through the paper in front of her. She was smiling when Alice returned and asked "What does it say?" as she popped the cosy over the teapot, and sat back down.

"It says here" replied Flo with a smirk "that no one is allowed to flush the toilet after ten o clock at night. Apparently the pipes rumble, and disturb the other guests" she paused and looked directly at Alice "One of our first jobs of the day is to flush them from top to bottom, that'll be your job"

Alice pulled a face "I thought we agreed I wasn't doing toilets?"

"We agreed *nowt!* and let's have it right, you said you didn't want to clean toilets, nowt was mentioned about not wanting to flush 'em"

"But why me?"

"Because, it says here, that Mr Basker did that job, and *you're* covering for *him*" Flo gave a triumphant smirk

Alice folded her arms, a sulk was coming "I'm not going"

"You've said you will now, it's not just me you'd be letting down, it'll be one of your dearest friends"

"Who?"

"The bloody doctor. You daft sod. The first day I met you, you was going on about the 'soirees' you and your mam attended" She paused for effect "or was all that a lie"

"I do *not* tell lies, madam" said an indignant Alice, and she grimaced "I heave flushing me own toilet, I can't do it"

"Okay" snapped Flo, fed up of her moaning "We'll take turns"

"I'll be sick"

"You'll be in the right place then won't you? just shurrup, we'll sort it when we get there"

Alice smirked victoriously and changed the subject "So, where will we be living?"

"In the housekeeper and her husband's rooms, obviously! Makes sense seeing as they're both stuck in the hospital with a broken leg apiece. Mrs Howarth said they're lovely rooms, and on the ground floor too, just off the kitchen. I'm just glad they're not in the cellar, my friend Annie, went 'into service' at a big house in Sheffield and the servants quarters were in the basement, even the Butler's rooms! I hate feeling locked in, I only lock the door if I can't pay the Club man" She read on some more. "*And,* we've got our own bathroom...Indoors!..but, the staff can use it during the day"

"Oh great" said Alice, her voice oozing sarcasm "full use of a public lavatory" Flo tutted, best friend or not, she was hard bloody work sometimes. "Don't be daft there's only four of em! ...and Philip when he comes...and the gardener on a Monday and Thursday...and maybe the window cleaner, 'cos he's here a while. I had more than that using the loo when me and Bob had our wedding do back at the house"

"You're not as fussy as me" sniffed Alice. "I'll be keeping a flannel and some bleach in there" Flo rolled her eyes, and carried on,

"He does inside and out, does the window cleaner, and one of us has to stay with him when he does the guest's inside windows. You can have the pleasure of that job, you're good at not trusting people, and letting em know it!"

Alice gave her friend a dirty look "And *what* else does it say?"

"Well, you'll be pleased to know that we've both got our own bedroom, 'cos I bloody am! We've got a sitting room too with a little kitchenette bit so we can brew up. without having to traipse to the big kitchen at night *And*, you're not gonna believe this" she said excitedly "there's a telly! It's their silver wedding anniversary gift from the doctor and his wife, earlier this year. And also, as the doctor told me, for their excellent service, second only to mine if I'd been there. The doctor's words *not* mine" she replied in answer to Alice's gurning. "they were dead good to me too, when I worked for them, never got me a telly though. Mind you, I don't think they were properly invented then, aw, remember them sorting out the car for me wedding?" she didn't wait for a reply "We can watch telly *every* night Alice, int it exciting?"

"I prefer the radio" said a sullen Alice

"You won't after a week" replied a cheery Flo

"But I wanted to go out and about a bit, not sit staring at a telly. It won't last this telly palaver, people will soon realise it's daft. I mean, you don't write a book on a postage stamp when you've got bigger pieces of paper, *Why* watch a film on such a small screen, when you can see it on a massive one at the pictures?

"Say that again after a week of telly" said Flo dismissively "Anyway, you'll have plenty of opportunities to get out and about, 'cos it's our job to get the daily shopping. The fresh stuff like bread and veg, everything else is delivered"

"I'm not lugging a dozen loaves up the street every day!" retorted Alice

"You won't have to, I'll carry six"

"I'm serious Flo"

"So am I" Flo was getting frustrated with her friends constant whinging "look" she snapped "we'll have to manage, neither of us can drive so Mr. Basker's little van is as much use as a chocolate teapot! Mrs Lomas from Hinde street has eight kids to shop for, and she does it with three or four of 'em in tow, we've only got six guests, two of em go away every weekend so, that's two less dinners-

"I *can* count!"

"I'm just getting it straight, 'cos you'll go round the houses annoying me. We can manage, we're still in our prime"

"Yes, but some of us, aren't used to manual labour like

some who clean houses all day long for a living. *Some* of us have independent means and if they *did* choose to work, they'd be a Secretary somewhere posh"

"Well, *some* people had better pull their socks up, before we go, 'cos I can't see an ability to type fifty words of nonsense, in a minute, coming in handy when the cooker's not working and a dozen people are waiting for breakfast. In fact! I think that, *some* people should *shut their gobs* or they'll be going nowhere, 'cos unlike *some* people, I *do* have other friends"

Alice was tempted to say *"See if I care"* and storm out, but, she did *care.* Life had got a bit boring since the excitement of 'The War' this was an opportunity to get away from boring Moston, for a bit, *and* spend time with her best friend.

The remaining days flew by, and even with Alice's faffing and constant complaining, the day soon arrived for them to leave for the guest house.

CHAPTER 4

Flo and Bob said their goodbyes early, he was off to one of his jobs and wouldn't be back until she'd gone. He'd shrugged off her concerns *"Are you sure you can manage?"* with a brusque *"I was managing before you were born"* He didn't mean it in a mean way and Flo knew it, she gave him a loving kiss and off he went.

She'd said her 'byes to Joyce too, who was quite looking forward to spending time alone with Dad, she always got on better with him than her Mam. Joyce had set off for work wondering what to make for tea that night, Mam had left a list, but she was gonna ignore it *"Just cos it's a Friday why do we have to eat fish?"* Neither her nor Dad liked fish much, but it was 'the law' according to Mam. '*I'm gonna make a cheese and onion pie'* she thought defiantly.

Not too long after the two most precious people in her life had said goodbye, Alice arrived with two medium sized suitcase, and out of breath.

"It was murder carting them over the cobbles"

"Why didn't you come the main road way?"

"Too long"

"*What?* by about three foot, you daft sod!" Flo shook her

head and Alice turned to go back up the lobby. "*Where* are you going *now*?"

"Back home to get the last case"

Flo looked down at her own luggage, one suitcase and a large handbag for the bits that wouldn't fit in "What the bleedin' ell are you bringing? your entire house?"

"I'm not leaving anything that Joan can root through I've stuck hair on me bedroom door 'an all,and it better be there when I come back"

"Come again?" said Flo, in utter disbelief

"It was in a book I read about a detective, he put hair on the door to find out if someone was going in there.,turned out to be the butler"

"You're not normal! anyway hurry up the taxis due in an hour and I need to tidy up before we go"

She'd cleared away the pots and was just sweeping the carpet when Alice returned, with an even bigger suitcase.

"What on earth have you got in that?"

"Stuff!"

"Let me see?"

"Why should I?"

"Because, you won't be going if you don't" said an

increasingly fed up Flo. Alice tutted and reluctantly opened the case, Flo couldn't believe her eyes "You know when I joked about the kitchen sink?"

"Yeah" replied Alice, sarcastically "Why? Can you see one?"

"No, but *why* have you brought a washbasin and jug? There are *sinks*!"

"It was me Gran's, and it's an antique, I don't want it getting broken, she falls over her own feet does Joan" Flo gave her friend the dirtiest of looks "Either *it* stays here or you do! I'm starting to regret this already" She sighed

"Well, I'm not taking it home, can I put it in your cupboard?"

"You can put it in a pipe and smoke it, for all I care, as long as it doesn't come with *us*"

She spotted something else as Alice was removing the wash basin "And what the bloody ell is *THAT*?" she screamed, spotting what she thought was a pillow, "there's no need to bring your own pillow. They do *have* bedding"

"it's not a pillow"

"well, what else does anyone put in a pillowcase?"

"Oh, that's just me important paperwork"

"Y'what? said a stunned Flo "you've brought enough paper to fill a pillow? are you mental?"

"It's alright for you" said Alice sulkily, "you haven't got nosy Joan from next door opening and closing your curtains every day for four weeks"

"Keep them on top of the wardrobe like everyone else. Joan's nosy about goings on, not letters from the corporation she'd never root that much. Plus she's only four foot nothing, how could she reach?"

"I've seen ladders in her back yard"

"You're not normal! What else have you got in there? Glenn Miller? Amy Johnson?"

"Ha, ha" said Alice, realising she was being teased..

The remaining time before the taxi arrived was filled by frantic tidying up and double checking that they both had everything they needed. At one o clock on the dot, they heard a knock on the door, their taxi had arrived. It was time for the adventure to begin. They eagerly clambered into the cab and waved goodbye to the house.

A bus journey to the south Manchester suburb of Didsbury, that would have taken a good hour, was completed in less than twenty minutes by taxi. Both ladies, excited at what lay ahead, sat quietly in the back of the cab, unusually reticent as the taxi driver chatted away. Even his revelation that he'd once had Robert Donat in his taxi, and he was a mean tipper, failed to garner much response, other than for Flo to comment that she'd loved him in *Mr chips*. Alice kept quiet, mainly because she suffered from travel sickness on anything smaller than a 'sharra' When the taxi reached it's destination she was quite green.

The Cab, as instructed, dropped them off, on the corner. Flo, opened the envelope marked 'taxi fare' and found more than enough to pay him so, she added a generous tip and he all but flew out of his cab to assist the ladies with their bags. Alice made an indignant sound, you could get bread for a week, with what Flo had just given him, on top of the extortionate fare. The only thing that stopped her from saying anything was the fact, it wasn't her money being spent, and the warning look on Flo's face. The 'look' on Alice's face had Flo reluctantly assisting by taking one of her suitcases -the smallest one. They walked a few yards up the tree lined road and there it was, home and work for the next four weeks. *I've worked in worse surroundings,* thought Flo, smiling as she took in the view.

"Innit lovely Alice?"

Begrudgingly, Alice had to agree, she'd half hoped it wouldn't live up to Flo's expectations. "It looks okay" she shrugged. "Is that rising damp on the gable end?"Flo rolled her eyes. "that's you all over, int it? never mind taking in the lovely surroundings" She paused to look around her, then continued her rant "With *trees!* all you wanna do is find summat to moan about. I'm sorry I brought you, now"

Knowing Flo was more than capable of changing her mind, and not wanting to get the next bus back to 'Town' Alice wisely decided to keep her mouth shut, for a few seconds at least. "I wasn't moaning" she said brightly, having suddenly had a brainwave. "I was doing my job" she looked at Flo with an air of smugness. "I'm here to cover for the housekeeper's husband aren't I?" she didn't wait for Flo to respond "I'm sure maintenance of the building is amongst his duties?" Flo, briefly contemplated punching the smirk off Alice's face, but, decided it wasn't worth it. She chose to ignore her and stepped back a bit to survey her new 'kingdom'

Set in its own brick walled grounds, only the right hand side of the building was visible from the road, framed by a pair of elaborate and large black wrought iron gates, kept permanently open for the convenience of guests with cars, which currently stood at two, neither of whom were 'home' at this time. It was also the entrance for tradesmen, who had ample room on the gravel driveway to get through to the rear of the house, where deliveries and staff entered at all times.

A few feet to the left of the gates, was the pedestrian entrance, another black wrought iron gate, but this time, the size of Flo's back gate, maybe a little taller, but not much. On the wall that divided the gates hung a white wooden sign, etched in posh black lettering. "It looks like the first page of a posh bible" said Flo admiringly and she read aloud what was written on it,

OAKENELM GUEST HOUSE

Superior rooms for refined Ladies and Gentlemen

Breakfast and evening meals

Residents lounge and Dining room

Suited to persons working in the medical profession

Long stays only

All enquiries to Mrs Basker (Housekeeper) Telephone Didsbury 343 or kindly enquire at reception

Tradesmen and staff to the rear

We're not staff yet, though are we? she thought.

"Come on Alice, let's take the scenic route, she twisted the latch, and pushed open the gate.

Because of the well kept, and very tall hedge to the right hand side, dividing the pathway from the rest of the garden, and the boundary wall to the left, almost concealed by climbing plants, plus a neat row of trees, from which the guest house got its name, the house itself, was invisible until you'd walked seven or so paces of the curving, flagged pathway. Both ladies caught their breath, as it came into view

"Bloody lovely" sighed Flo as they both gazed in awe at the scene ahead of them. The path had brought them out to a large paved courtyard, with plants of various colours in large stone planters. At a jaunty angle to these pots was a statue of a girl in a toga carrying a jug, and at the gable end, stood a black wooden gate, *that'll be the staff entrance* thought Flo, referring in her head, to the plan left by the Howarths

"Oh my bloomin' God!" exclaimed Alice "we're living in a house with statues in the garden, mind you, I'm used to it" she quickly composed herself as Flo laughed "Your pot lions don't ever come close luv, stop kidding yourself" but, she was impressed too. The path had brought them out to the far left of the house's frontage. Alice quickly estimated it looked the length of about six houses on her street, and was suitably impressed. Large bay widows, with sparkling clean glass, jutted out at regular intervals,three to the left of what seemed to be the front entrance and one to the right of it

As they turned to walk towards the main entrance, they got their first glimpse of the main grounds, and it really took their breath away

Hidden behind the wall that bore the signage, and the pathway hedge was an immaculate lawn, at least four times the size of Flo or Alice's backyards

"You could play bowls on that" exclaimed Alice. "and look at them benches, it's like a mini Picadilly Gardens"

Flo couldn't help but agree. Dotted around the lawn were circular and oval flower beds, bursting with colour and a variety of foliage. She felt lucky to be here at this time of year, when the garden was at its finest, she was at heart a country girl and looked forward for the first time in years to waking up to a garden view, instead of the usual back gate and someone tall's head bobbing past the gate as they clopped up the entry. She was also looking forward to meeting Fred the Gardener, who would be tending the garden every Monday and Thursday according to the Staff list she'd been given. She admired people who did a good job, no point doing something, if you weren't going to do it well.

She looked around for Alice who had found a sundial atop a stone pedestal, a short way away, stood a similar stone pedestal bearing the weight of a bird bath, she beckoned to Flo, excitedly. "Look at this Flo. If anyone else around our way, says they've stayed somewhere with a sundial, I'll call 'em a liar to their face" She stared at the sundial intently. "I've not got a clue how they work though, have you?"

"Have I eck" snorted Flo. "but, they can't be that good or no-one would have invented watches. Looks lovely though. Anyway, come on. Let's go in and introduce ourselves. I wonder if their Philip still recognises me? It's been a good few years since he saw me"

"You look as haggard now as you did then, and you've got the same hairstyle, he'll remember"

"Do you want to go home?" said Flo indignantly and Alice wisely decided to shut up, following on in silence as Flo headed towards the front door.

The entrance to the guest house was in keeping with its surroundings, a large black door with brass doorknob and letterbox and two arched stained glass inserts. The two wide steps leading up to it, had been freshly swept and two stone planters filled with summer blooms stood either side of the door "Come on then" said Flo "let's make ourselves known"

The door as expected was unlocked, which miffed Alice a bit, cos she loved ringing doorbells and the one to the right of the door was a particularly posh one, large round shiny brass with a tempting push button. Alice loved to push buttons in more ways than one "Aw, I love pushing buttons" she sighed. When it came to 'pushing buttons' she was an expert.

As they entered the guest house, they were greeted by a vision of loveliness, the reception area was completely carpeted, and dotted about, there was a tasteful mix of easy chairs, three in total, each with an oak side table, A sideboard adorned with magazines and information leaflets stood against the wall immediately to the left of the front door, to the right of the door, stood a coat stand and beneath it a container for umbrellas. Further to the right was a large imposing reception desk, currently empty, and before them lay a staircase visible as far as the first floor, like all the wood in the building the staircase was oak and well polished. To the right of the staircase was a nook which housed a public telephone, *How convenient* thought Flo, *'its a pity I don't know anyone with a phone, 'cept Bob's sister, but, it'd be a foggy day in hell, the day I'd ring her'* To the left of the staircase was a wide corridor which Flo knew led to the residents lounge and dining areas. "I'm gonna like it here" said Alice with a satisfied sigh, *'we'll see'* thought Flo as they approached the reception desk, still unmanned, where a shiny brass bell instructed them to *'ring for attention'* "go on then you childish sod" said Flo. Alice dinged the bell , and the door to the rear of reception, already slightly ajar flew open and out came a tall, well dressed young man in his mid twenties

"Well, you've grown" said Flo with a wink, to the tall young man stood before her. "Florrie" he exclaimed and rushed out from behind the desk to give her a big hug, he'd loved Flo from the moment she'd come to live with them with them, she'd sneak him an extra rasher and said not a word to his parents, when she'd found his stash of rude comics. Even if she *had* binned them.

"Let me look at you then?"said Flo, pulling away from his

embrace and holding him at arm's length "Well, you've certainly got taller, and even more handsome" she said with a smile, she meant it too.

Philip blushed, at six foot tall a slim build, with dark brown hair and an attractive face, he truly was a handsome lad, but, severely lacking in confidence especially with the opposite sex

"He puts me in mind of a brunette Leslie Howard with a bit of David Niven if he didn't have a 'tache" Flo would later remark

"You've not changed a bit either, Florrie"

"Oh, g'way with yourself" said Flo, with good humour. I've put on a good couple of stone since I last saw you. And *don't* call me Florrie, you're big enough to call me Flo now. She didn't add that she hated being called Florrie, and shot Alice a warning glance, not to mention it too. She turned back to Philip "You remember Alice - Miss Shufflebottom who become Mrs Clough, don't you?"

He did and his reply reflected this, with a terse but polite *hello,* accompanied by a handshake, Alice wasn't getting a hug, he remembered the sly nips she'd given him when Flo wasn't looking. After the greetings were done Philip suggested that the ladies settle in their living quarters first before joining him for a late lunch and a tour of the guest house. He directed them to the corridor on the right of the staircase, that led to the staff section of the large house, a sign on the wall, politely barring guests from going beyond this point.

About ten paces down the long corridor, he pointed out the back door to the grounds, and entrance for staff. A little further along he pointed out, somewhat embarrassed, the bathroom that was for their use. They didn't go in. To the right and a little further up were the double doors leading to the kitchen, they could hear the staff talking and the clanging of pans.Philip pointed out the obvious, "That's the kitchen Ladies, but we'll meet the staff later, once you're settled" and they carried on down the corridor for a few more steps, until they came to a door marked *Private.* he took out a key and opened the door to Flo and Alice's home for the next four weeks."these are your quarters" he said with a smile

Both women were very impressed by what they saw. Mrs Basker was obviously immaculate.

Briefly pointing out the amenities "that's the kitchenette area, and those doors on the right hand wall are the bedrooms" Philip suggested they unpack and get their bearings before joining him in "Should we say half an hour?" in the office, where he reminded them they would be having something to eat. After a hug from Flo and a nod of the head from Alice, he left them to settle in, "straight down the corridor all the way" he replied to Alice's comment "you could get lost in here" and with that he took his leave.

Once alone, both women stood for a moment, taking it all in, until Alice broke the silence with "So, are we gonna have a root? and which one is my bedroom?"

Flo didn't really hear her, she was transfixed by the telly in the corner.

CHAPTER 5

Flo, finally broken free from the spell of the television, sat down at the table and pulled out her notes "It say's here that your room is the one on the far right"

"Any reason?" questioned Alice

"yeah, the one I have, is the master bedroom and has the telephone in it, and it sometimes rings late or early hours"

"Fine with me" replied her friend "it's hard enough for me to drop off in the first place, I couldn't be doing with the ringing of a phone" but, that was before she saw her room, Flo ignored her, knowing what was to come, Mrs Howarth had already warned her about the second bedroom so, she attempted to delay the inevitable "what do you think about the living room?" she asked. Alice looked around her, spotlessly clean, no complaints there. The living area to the right was divided from the kitchenette by the Formica table they were sat at. In the corner to the left stood a small sink, next to a small table holding a two ring electric cooker and a kettle. Pots and pans were stored in a small Welsh dresser further along the wall, and on its main shelf stood a tray with their beloved brewing up tackle, sat on it.

The living area was slightly cramped but cosy, a floral three piece suite with a coffee table in front, surrounded the television, which stood majestically in the corner, just beyond the door that led to Flo's bedroom. A mixture of ornaments, not all to the ladies' tastes, were dotted along the tiled mantle- piece and beneath it was a fire already laid ready to be lit if needed, but, for the cold mornings when time was of the essence, a small electric heater stood at the side next to the companion set.

"The wallpaper's a bit horrible but, it'll do" Alice said, somewhat condescendingly "it's better than distemper!" retorted Flo, referring to the decor in Alice's back bedroom. "I'm getting that done soon" snapped back her friend "I'll give her this much though" she continued, meaning the currently bed bound housekeeper "she's a good housekeeper, the place is spotless. Let's have a look at the bedrooms now, cos we need to meet Philip in a few minutes, and I won't lie, I'm starving, me tummy thinks me throat's been cut" Flo sighed, picked her case and bag up, and headed for her own bedroom, she knew what was coming next

She was pleasantly surprised at the housekeeper's bedroom, a double bed freshly made, sat square in the middle of the back wall, either side of it was a small table with green shaded table lamps adorning the tops. On the right hand table,there also stood a black Bakelite phone identical to those she saw in films and her 'posh' ladies' homes. On the opposite wall stood a wardrobe and matching dressing table, a quick peek inside revealed the two top drawers had been emptied, has had half the wardrobe, if not more, for only two suits and three dresses, showing the couple to be both short and slim, hung in it. The top of the wardrobe held two large suitcases, Flo stood on tip toes and grabbed the handle of one, they were both full. *'probably their stuff'* she thought to herself. After pulling drawers open she couldn't see where the clean bed linen was stored and made a mental note to ask Philip, then she glanced at her watch and realised it was nearly time to meet him. *'I'll sort my luggage out afterwards'* she thought, and turned to leave the room just as Alice came storming in.

"Oh, I see someone's got the right end of the donkey" she spat, looking round the room. Her voice got higher "have you seen where I'm expected to sleep? have ya?"

"How could I you daft sod" replied Flo neglecting to say that Bob had pointed out it was a *small* room, when he'd looked over the plans "we both got here at the same time, anyway, what's up?" she continued, feigning innocence "Go and look at my so called bedroom, then see if you want to ask me 'what's up' again" said Alice bitterly, Flo suppressed a smirk and headed for the other bedroom. "Aw, innit cosy" she said, still doing her best to keep the smirk from spreading on her face.

"*COSY?*" shrieked Alice. I've got more roomy button tins!"

"I don't understand your problem" said Flo "You've got a clean bed, a wardrobe and chest of drawers" her eyes darted around some more "Lovely curtains, and a matching eiderdown, what more do you want?"

"A bit of space to move about would be a help" retorted Alice, sarcasm oozing from every pore "I'll have to walk sideways to get in bed"

"Well, you're only little" said Flo dismissively, and look at this way, your star sign is the Crab. It's like 'fate' brought you here"

"No it's not. I'm a Gemini"

"Which one's that?"

"The Twins!" Alice tutted at her friends ignorance.

"Oh yeah, the two-faced one, well, you know me and star signs" Flo huffed "Load of rubbish"

"Say's someone who knocks on to drag me round the corner 'cos she's seen a magpie?" answered Alice, apoplectic at *the cheek of it!* "Gordon whatisface! look at the time" said Flo, trying to change the subject, they'd be here all day if she didn't put a stop to Alice's moaning "I don't know about you but, I'm spitting feathers and I could murder a brew, come on, we'll sort all this out later on" she headed towards the door without waiting for an answer. Alice, suddenly realising she was spitting feathers too, mumbled to herself *"I'll be having words about this"* and followed her friend out of the door.

As they strolled back up the corridor, Alice decided she

needed the toilet, and after reassurance that Flo would wait for her, because she feared being trapped forever in never ending lobbies, she entered the bathroom to spend a penny. Just as everywhere else she'd seen so far, she could find no fault with this room. Black and white tiled floors, all four walls half tiled in white, with a pleasant light green paint on the walls. A sink, bath and toilet in sparkling white, all flush against the wall forming an L-shape, completed the look, alongside a stack of white towels atop a small freestanding cupboard between bath and sink.

"Are you still there?" she shouted to Flo

"No, I've gone to Timbukto" shouted a sarcastic Flo, through the bathroom door. Alice tutted.

As she stood waiting for Alice, Flo looked up and down the corridor, she knew if you went straight on, it led to the dining room, a sharp left just before that, brought you back to reception, the way Phillip had first escorted them. She made mental notes in her head *that's the kitchen doors, to me left, to the right that's the back door*

Suddenly noticing a door sized indentation a little further up, she walked up to it. It *was* a door, or more specifically it had once *been* a door. The door itself was still there, but the door knob had been removed and unlike all the others doors that were their natural shade, this had been painted the same mid green as the walls, as if to camouflage it. Just then, Alice came out of the bathroom, and seeing Flo further up the corridor, said with an air of indignation "I knew you'd leave me!"

"Oh shut up" snapped Flo. She'd gone at least two hours without a brew, and she was feeling moody" come on or Philip will think we've got lost" *I wish you'd get lost and stop being bossy'* thought Alice but, said nothing. As they reached reception Flo noticed that Alice was carrying her handbag. "why are you bringing your handbag? we're where we live! That's like going in the kitchen from the parlour of your own house and taking your handbag with you" Alice, wondering if Flo had clocked on to her habit of taking her handbag to the toilet in her own house, replied in an offended tone "I've brought *my* bag cos its got my notebook and pen. We *agreed* that I'd take notes at the meeting, so *pardon me* for being professional" She finished with a snooty look aimed at her friend

"What meeting?" said Flo, confused. "the one we're going to now. I did that secretarial course remember?"

"You did a week" snorted Flo "and left 'cos you didn't like it" She sighed "make notes if you want but, stop going on like you're Katherine Hepburn, you'll be wearing 'slacks' next" In a deliberately terse tone Alice replied "I don't bloody think so!" but, as they were right outside the office Flo ignored her and pushed open the door with a cheery "Cooey, it's only us" Philip looked up from his desk and smiled. "you must be hungry and in need of a cup of tea" he said, directing them to sit down at the small dining table in the corner, where there, sat a pot of tea, steam rising from its spout, and a selection of sandwiches and cake.

Her companions, both agreed when Flo pushed her empty plate aside and declared "I hadn't realised how hungry I was" after the three of them had demolished several sandwiches and at least two French fancies apiece, whilst catching up on the missing years. After assuring Flo and Alice that there was no need to tidy up, as Beryl the cook's assistant would be in shortly to collect the pots, a pleasantly pleased Flo and especially Alice, sat down with Philip at his desk, to go over the things they needed to know. As Philip shuffled through his paperwork, Alice took out her note pad and licked the tip of her pencil ready for secretarial action. Flo wanted to kick her!

Double checking that Flo had her list of staff names and responsibilities, Philip began by arranging a chat sometime over the weekend regarding staff, for now it was more important to go over the rules for guests. Alice made her first notebook entry, *Meeting with Philip, either Saturday or Sunday to discuss our staff* Flo rolled her eyes. Alice ignored her, and Philip continued "e've found that a successful guest house, thrives on routine, and certain rules" The ladies listened intently, Alice occasionally jotting something down. "meal times are one such routine we adhere to. Breakfast is served from seven to eight o clock Monday to Friday and from eight til ten at weekends, we rarely have more than three guests in residence at weekends, but, I'll go through that with you later" He went back to mealtimes "we don't provide lunch, during the week, as all our guests work, during holidays and so forth, but, we will provide a lunch of sandwiches and cake if requested and ordered in advance, by guests on holiday or off work sick, for example"

"Sounds fair enough" agreed Flo. Philip smiled and continued "dinner is served between seven and eight in the evening, except Sunday's when Maureen is off, and we serve a two o clock lunch on that day, all prepared beforehand by her and Beryl, we simply stick it in the oven, and as I've previously said, most of our guests go away for the weekend. Serving at this time also means, you get the rest of the afternoon off, your only other commitment to the guests, being cocoa at suppertime. Weekday dinners are our busiest time, but Cook and her assistant are here til they finish, and there is very little to wash on a Sunday" Alice smiled at the thought of not having to wash pots after strangers had eaten off them. Flo mentally reminded herself, that when he said 'dinner' he meant 'tea'. "Supper *is* your responsibility though" he continued, and Alice's face dropped a little before he added, "but, it's simply cocoa and biscuits, served in the residents lounge" and her smile came back.

Shuffling through his papers again Philip exclaimed "Ah! that's what I was looking for. The most important thing I need to tell you, is, we have a new guest arriving on Monday evening, he will phone prior to arrival, but, its expected to be between six and seven. He won't require dinner, Maureen is aware, and his room is ready, I'll show you which one when we do the tour" He glanced back at his notes "His name is Dr Khatta, pronounced Carter. Should I spell that for you?" he said to Alice, noting she was writing it down. Alice looked at him like he was stupid "No thank you" she said tersely. In her head she thought *I can bloody spell, you know!*'

After a few moments of silence from Philip as he shuffled through paperwork, Alice sitting poised with pen and pad said "Is there anything else?" Her tone was irritating, Flo wanted to poke her in the eye. "erm, no, not for now" replied Philip. "I'll go over the staff duties after you've met them. I think we can start the grand tour now, he smiled as he stood up and gestured to the door "If you'd care to follow me, we'll start by meeting the staff" he glanced at the wall clock "and they're on their tea-break, so, back to the kitchen we go"

CHAPTER 6

On the way back to the kitchen, Flo noticed the camouflaged door again, now, didn't seem the appropriate time to ask about it but, she would, whenever she got a minute. Philip led them back into the kitchen, where four women sat round the large table, drinking tea, they all smiled when Philip and the ladies came in. '*he's a chip off the old block when it comes to treating people right'* thought Flo, and she made another mental note to find out why such a pleasant lad wasn't courting if not married by now. During their goodbye's on Flo's doorstep, Mrs Howarth had informed her that there was no upcoming marriage on the cards for Philip, she'd said it with an air of disappointment. Thinking back to their chats in the days when Flo 'lived in' reminded her of how much Mrs Howarth had looked forward to grandchildren in the years to come. Like Joyce, Philip was an only child. Like Flo, the doctor's wife had problems with her '*down belows'* Flo understood her desire for grandchildren, *she* wanted ten. She made yet another mental note '*I suppose Lawrence will have to do. I just hope me future grandkids don't have his eyes'.* they were *peepy* and made him look sly.

The oldest of the women, and obviously the cook, stood up and said "Hello my dears, welcome to the Asylum" the other women all burst out laughing, Philip pretended to chide her

"Now then Maureen, don't be telling the ladies the truth, they'll run away" Another bout of laughter, and even a smile from Alice, as the threesome were invited to join the others at the table. With the offer of tea politely refused *"We've just had ours"* introductions were made.

As the most senior member of staff and absolute ruler in the kitchen, the first introduction was to Maureen Massey, the Cook who sat at the top of the table. A short woman, not slim, but,not fat, even Alice had seemed to tower over her when they'd passed each other earlier on. Maureen had blonde, greying, curly hair held in some form of neatness by lots of visible kirby grips and some sort of cap a bit like a nurses cap. Every now and again a curl would ping out, to be hastily pushed back in with another kirby grip, Alice would later remark *"She looks like a fifty year old Shirley Temple"* She wore the same black dress, as worn by all the staff, with a full, white and un-frilled apron. She'd been the cook now for eight years and knew the kitchen like the back of her hand, she assured Flo and Alice that they need not worry about feeding the guests, she had it all in hand, another sigh of relief swept over the ladies, in three days they'd be in charge on their own, with Philip more than thirty miles away, contactable by telephone, but what use was that? The more the others could do, the better.

On Maureen's left sat Liz *'Don't call me Elizabeth, I hate it'* Cathcart, the chambermaid of ten years. Second only to

Mr and Mrs Basker in length of service,she had a warm
and friendly air about her. Average height and slim build,
she looked to be in her early forties, her brown as yet
ungreying wavy hair, shoulder length when loose was tied
back in a neat chignon. She was dressed in her maids
uniform, of black short sleeved dress, the hem, a good
three inches below the knee, with crisp white pocketed
and frilled apron and a quite impractical white cap,
perched on the back of her head, but, it complimented
the uniform perfectly.

The professional approach of staff like Liz was another
factor in the guest house's success, and much valued by
the guests.

 Widowed with no children, her husband was killed in the
war, she was assisted in her job by a young girl called Lily,
who was sat on her immediate left. Lily worked Mondays,
Wednesdays, and Fridays, and lived not far from the guest
house, in Withington, with her parents and siblings. She
went by the title of assistant chambermaid and wore a
similar uniform to Liz, but devoid of frills, which were
obviously a sign of seniority amongst chambermaids.

"Oh I'm widowed too" Alice had piped up when Liz was
first introduced *"great innit?"*

Liz had bitten her lip. '*What a horror*' she'd thought. She
still wasn't over the loss of her Thomas, They'd only been
wed three weeks when he was killed. She'd gone 'home'
after he died, and still lived with her elderly but active

parents, one bus away from Oakenhelm, She normally worked six days a week, but had agreed to work Sundays if needed, until the Baskers returned. It wasn't hard to say yes to a request for help, from the doctor and his wife, they were wonderful employers, treating all the staff with respect, regardless of station.

Opposite Liz sat Beryl, a plump teenager and the tallest of the three, at five foot seven. She had long black, straight hair, tied up in a pony tail, that flared out beneath her cap like a horses tail. The same dress as the others but with a plain white half apron. Her job was to help the cook in all areas, and on occasion assist if needed in other areas. If a guest spilled something in their room, it was Beryl that cleaned it up, it was Beryl that collected the pots after dinner, and it was Beryl that made up the fires, including the one in the housekeeper's rooms. A fact Flo came to appreciate after a long day and facing a chilly summer's evening. It was also Beryl, to Alice's relief whose first job of the day, was to wash the breakfast pots, serving and collecting the pots being the only requirements of the housekeeper. Maureen's niece by marriage, but someone she had real affection for, Beryl was what people called 'Away with the fairies' in decades to come it would be termed learning difficulties, but,Doctor Howarth had had no hesitation in offering her a job, as unlike some, he knew she could work well under supervision. She knew her work routine to a T and she came and went with Auntie Maureen, so she wasn't scared to come here. She couldn't go to places on her own, she got lost and scared and mean people laughed at her. Flo took an instant like to her. Alice knew she was going to get on her nerves.

When alone with Flo, later that day, Maureen had confided in her "*You've no worries with our Beryl when it comes down to doing what's she's supposed to do but, if you ask her the time you'll have to remind her what a watch is*"

Another reason behind the success of the guest house, and its ability to retain good staff were the extra perks they got. Every year the whole staff were given their own *Wakes* week, whilst the doctor, his wife and son ran the guest house with the help of agency staff. The date was flexible according to how many guests were in residence, but it was always April or May. As an added bonus fellow guest house owners in Southport, and good friends of the Howarths provided half board accommodation at half price for the staff and their families. An offer they all usually took up, further cementing the bond they had both as staff members and friends. Doctor Howarth wasn't daft, happy staff meant excellent service, which, combined with the warm and friendly atmosphere, was the secret of Oakenhelm's success

It was time for Maureen to make a start on that evening's dinner and time for Philip to show the ladies more of the guest house. A quick *Cheerio* to everyone and they continued the tour, carrying on, past the exit to reception, which brought them to a door that led directly to the dining room. Philip explained that all meals served in the dining room were brought via this route. "We *never* take food through the reception area" he stressed "We have high standards"

The dining room was more proof of those high standards, wood paneled on all four wall and filled with brass wall plaques. Alice rolled her eyes and thought *'no way am I doing brass'* Flo thought *'I'll put Alice on brass'* To their immediate right, along the wall was a long sideboard, containing fresh linen and table settings, its wide top used for the serving trays in the morning.which had individual compartments containing bacon, sausages, tomatoes, and eggs, as well as a platter of toast, a pot of porridge and box of cornflakes, alongside a large jug of milk.. Drinks were served by the housekeeper but guests helped themselves to food. Any leftovers were used by the staff for their mid-morning breakfast..

A large green marble fire surround, occupied a central position on the wall opposite, its fireplace already set for lighting if required, with a brass companion set to one side, and a set of large brass bells to the other.

Eight round tables with green under cloths and crisp white over cloths were scattered in a seemingly random but pleasing way, around the room. A posy of flowers from the garden, in crystal vases adorned each table as did the table settings of green and white crockery with silver cutlery. Each guest had a dedicated table according to their room number and the number of table settings needed for that table. Residents were allowed to have guests to dinner by prior arrangement and their bills were adjusted accordingly. The generous size of the dining room allowed for relative privacy for each guest, as they dined. Flo noticed that table one had place settings for two, whilst table two was empty except for its vase of flowers. She was sure her notes said both rooms were occupied. Philip explained that Misses Tippit and Barker always dined together. Alice raised an eyebrow.

On the back wall of the dining room, were two large, mainly glass doors framed by the same curtains that adorned the whole house, pale green in colour and bursting with darker green flowers and leaves. The doors led out to the private patio area, where there was no grass but, greenery was provided by tubs of flowers with wooden seats and small tables scattered about. To the bottom right of the patio, was a gate, mainly for the use of Fred the gardener, guests were kindly discouraged from going out this way, it led to the rear grounds of the guest house, Flo and Alice had briefly viewed the rear garden, earlier on from the back door. It contained Fred's shed, the laundry room and the lines for hanging out washing, as well as car parking space for the guest house van, operated by Mr Basker, and Philip's car which looked fancy, but not as fancy as his dad's

Back inside, Philip led them to the residents lounge, divided from the dining room on the opposite wall to the patio doors, by a pair of large doors, in solid oak, that opened out to the lounge, tastefully decorated in the

green that seemed to be the theme throughout the house.
The walls were decorated in a flocked and subtly striped
wallpaper and portraits of unknown people from days
gone by, adorned the walls. On one wall, stood the same
fireplace and surround as in the dining room, with the
addition of a mantle clock and several delicate statuettes
featuring 'crinolined' ladies, and arranged around the fire,
easy chairs and side tables with lamps completed the
furnishings in that side of the room. To the end furthest
from the dining room, curtains adorned the large bay
window, the view of the grounds as delightful as the
views from the upstairs rooms.

To the left of the bay window a gramophone stood on a
table, with a collection of records, mainly classical music.
On the other side was another table with a collection of
magazines placed next to a large bookcase filled with
books. Two easy chairs each with a standard lamp behind
it gave it the air of a designated reading area. *'It's like
having a library in your own house'* thought Alice,
impressed by all she'd seen so far... except her bedroom.

The room had an overall aura of calmness. Flo imagined
how lovely it would be in winter with the curtains drawn
and a roaring fire.

Both women were feeling decidedly better about the task
that lay ahead after meeting the staff, and undertaking the
downstairs tour. They'd meet Fred the gardener and
general handy man when he came in on Monday but,
judging by the grounds they'd have no problem with him

either, and he too had agreed to come in above his regular Monday, Thursday and every other Saturday if needed.

As they walked through the door closest to the window, they found themselves back in the reception area. Now they were headed for the upstairs rooms, and the chance for Flo and Alice to see what would be required of them...and have a nosy into the lives of the guests.

CHAPTER 7

It was a breathless duo who stood by a not at all breathless Philip outside a door on the second floor.

"We'll be alright in a minute" gasped Flo, "we're just not used to it. you've got a *lot* of stairs"

"It's like Blackpool Tower" panted Alice making over exaggerated gasping sounds. "well, there are just six more behind this door to the attic room" chuckled Philip, he'd long gotten used to the steep stairs, spread over three floors. And for this reason rooms at the top were always reserved for the younger guests. He went to open the door leading to the attic steps for room eight but, Flo put her hand on his, her other clutching her chest "give us a minute, Philip luv" she wheezed "I'm not bothered about the stairs, we'll manage 'em but I'll be going at a slower pace than you. We ran up them stairs quicker than Jesse Owens" she added, to herself "*I could do with a cig*"

Philip smiled and held out his hands, in a gesture of apology, and whilst the two women got their breath back, he told them about who resided there "Our guest in this room" he said "is a Miss Sally Henderson, she works in the records department of the hospital" only Flo noticed him blush slightly as he said her name. The ladies had now recovered, after a fashion! So, he led them up the six steps and used his master key to open the door. Each guest had been informed, out of courtesy that the new managers would be given a brief tour of their rooms, none had objected, but, he *had* noticed that Miss Henderson had seemed a tad concerned. He had no idea why, her room was immaculately clean and pristine. Philip pointed to a photograph on the neat dressing table, showing a young woman, stood next to who were presumably her parents. The resemblance between her and both her parents was undeniable, but as they were both dark haired, she looked a little odd, stood next to them, with her blonde hair. Alice immediately thought *'THAT comes out of a bottle'* She looked shy too, but there was no doubting her prettiness, Flo would later have the feeling upon meeting her, that she didn't realise how pretty she was. A wise Flo, also noticed how much Philip liked her, again, she'd been the only one to spot his blush while pointing to the photograph of her. Her clothes looked a little old fashioned in what looked to be a recent picture, but, there was no disputing that she was a very attractive girl, blonde hair framing a heart shaped face, petite features and a shy smile, in contrast to the other people stood, next to hers, obviously family, but all dark haired and miserable looking. The thought going through Alice's head as she glanced at the photographs, was 's*eems like someone's 'Dad' was working away when his child was conceived'*

The only thing that seemed out of place to Flo, were the amount of mirrors in Sally's room. Judging by her photo, the lack of make -up or toiletries on her dressing table, and the dowdy dresses hung in her wardrobe - visible briefly when nosy Alice opened it with the excuse *"Oops! I thought it was a door"* Sally would seem to be a girl, not troubled by vanity, so why so many mirrors? Because in addition to the mirrors available in the room, a large one on the outer door of the wardrobe, and the three connected ones on the dressing table. The resident had added two floor standing ones, and three hand mirrors in varying sizes, lay neatly on the dressing table. *'Oh well, now so queer as folk'* thought Flo.

Other than the dearth of mirrors, the other thing that stuck out, was how neat and clean the room was, almost clinically clean."did you say she was a Nurse? Flo asked Philip "she works in the medical records department" he replied. "ell, working in a hospital must rub off on her, isn't she neat? She'd make someone a good wife" she said, looking 'innocently' at Philip, who blushed again, and this time, Alice noticed

"Are *you* married Philip?" She asked, knowing full well he wasn't

"Erm, no. Have you seen the view?" he spluttered, heading to the window. Like six of the other guest rooms, number eight was a front facing room, with magnificent views of the garden, and being at the highest point in the house, gifted a view that stretched to the horizon.

"Beautiful" the ladies murmured together...

Lily, the assistant chambermaid, loved the attic room too. She entered the room, each time, knowing full well the bed would be made, unless it was bed change day, then the sheets and pillowcases would be removed and placed neatly on the table to the side of the bed. Everywhere else would be spotless too, a brief tidy around was all the attic room ever needed. Sometimes Lily would just sit awhile, for one, to get her breath back after the climb and to stare out of the window at the houses in the distance, which were even *more* distant behind their own equally posh gates and the wide cobbled street, which was at least three times as wide as the streets around the home that she shared with Mum, Dad and eight siblings, of which she was the eldest. Liz knew how easy a job the attic room was too, but didn't begrudge Lily her breather, she was a hard working girl.

Regardless of the beautiful surroundings, Lily felt sorry for the people living here. Despite the comforts, both of surroundings and wealth, they were lonely. The ladies on the first floor, didn't even have a home to go to, this was *it* And despite the attentive attitude of the staff, for which they paid, no one mithered about them. If Lily was ten minutes late home, her mam had search parties out, especially on payday. *'It's nowt more than posh lodgings'* she often thought to herself.

Just before they left the attic room, Philip pointed out that they may have noticed all the curtains throughout the house were identical, this was to maintain a uniform and neat look, he explained. Changed twice a year during the spring and autumn cleans, heavy green velvet ones were the replacement for the winter months. Seeing Alice's face and knowing what she was thinking, Flo quipped "it's alright Alice luv, we'll be gone before the next lot need putting up" Philip stifled a smile and said "should we carry on?" and led the way to their next point of call.

Just as he was about to close the door, Flo noticed the same two bar electric heater as was in her rooms, and Philip explained that all the guest rooms had them as an addition to the radiators which were only on at specific times. The only working fireplaces in guest rooms were in rooms one and two, the other rooms being heated by central heating radiators, quite ugly things with unglamourous curves and a general air of clumsiness. Clever interior design tried its best by hiding them behind curtains, somewhat diminishing their purpose by not letting the heat in, so, as a consolation by the caring owner, all rooms were also furnished with a small modern steel two bar electric heater; to provide instant heat on chilly days.

They left the attic and Philip turned right, leading them into room seven, it was currently vacant but would be the room given to the new doctor, on his arrival on Monday. The ladies were very impressed both by the decor and furnishings. The room contained two single beds already made, with green brocade eiderdowns on top of crisp white sheets. A 'desk like' dressing table sat in the alcove of the bay window, small enough to not spoil the magnificent view of the gardens. At the side of each bed was a table that housed a lamp, and opposite a double wardrobe. In the corner stood a sink with a mirror and shelving for toiletries. The fireplace, obviously not in use, was the home of a brass peacock, it feather's fanned out. The complimentary electric fire to the side of it.

A brief look in number six, the room to the left as you came out of the attic, showed the exact same decor and furnishings with the exception of wall hangings. Each room had a theme for its decor, in seven it was Lions and Tigers, in the attic room, landscapes, and in this room it was horses. Several items on the bedside table and and mail on the dressing table, showed that this room was occupied, by a Mr Chad Hawkins. "Mr Hawkins is from America" explained Philip "and has about two more months with us. He's been overseeing the installation of medical equipment at the hospital, and he usually spends his weekends out and about exploring the country. He's off to see Hadrian's wall this weekend, so you'll get to meet him on Monday evening"

They left the American's room and Philip led them across the wide landing to what would turn out to be the bathroom, shared by the three rooms. He explained how all the floors had an identical layout, rooms to the front, bathrooms at the back, with the exception of room three, the only rear facing room on the first floor. For that reason, and it's size, it was the cheapest room to rent.

Although he knew no one was home, he knocked before entering, listened for a brief moment, and led them into the bathroom. Yet again the ladies were impressed at the sight before them.

A white freestanding bath, separated a toilet with chain flush, high cistern and varnished oak seat on one side, from a sink, with mirror and towel rail on the other. Philip opened a free standing cupboard to the right of the sink to reveal a stack of pristine white towels, and replacement sundries, to the left of the sink, stood a laundry basket for the disposal of used towels. A large window, frosted, and framed by a shorter version of the curtains, allowed plenty of natural light in, and was situated on the left hand side of the back wall, away from the fixtures and fittings further ensuing the privacy of guests. *'Oakenelm is a classy establishment'* thought Flo, as she stared approvingly at the black and white tiled floors and half tiled white walls, the upper walls painted in the same shade of light green as the housekeeper's bathroom.

Flo wondered what facilities were in place for the disposal of *'Time of the month'* stuff as she referred to Sanitary products. Both her and Alice, were *'due on'* in the next week or so. No problem for them as they had a fire in their rooms to dispose of the rags she'd brought with her, but, the girl in the attic room? What did she use? As bold as she was, she couldn't bring herself to ask Philip. For one, because she knew he'd be absolutely mortified and another, well, it just wasn't a subject for polite conversation. She could imagine Alice's response if having to empty bins with such things in.

"that's bloody disgusting! you should put them things in the outside bin yourself"

"you're not wrong Alice. I always know when you've got your little visitor, cos I hear my bin lid go"

"DO YOU MIND!"

"you started the conversation!"

Philip's voice interrupted her musings. "you may have read the instruction, not to flush the toilet after ten at night, this is why" he said, pulling the chain. It sounded like a large roar, accompanied by an orchestra of people chucking bricks. The trio held their hands to their ears until the noise lessened and the shaking stopped. *there's a price to be paid for luxury and laziness*, thought Flo to herself, grateful for once, of her own outside loo. Alice didn't keep *her* thoughts to herself

"Shouldn't you get someone to look at that? It doesn't sound normal to me. I've got an indoor lavatory and it doesn't sound nowt like that"

"Edwardian plumbing I'm afraid" replied Philip, apologetically

"Well, I wouldn't use them again"

"Erm, no - I meant"

"Don't bother luv" interrupted Flo, rolling her eyes at Alice's stupidity. "shall we move on?" she prompted Philip, "of course, of course" he replied still bemused at Alice's comment. "follow me ladies" and he led them down to the next floor.

Everything on the second floor was identical, with the exception of the wall hangings, paintings of cottages in room six, currently unoccupied, and the room Philip was going to stay in over the weekends, during Flo and Alice's tenure.

In room five, the theme was still lifes, this room was occupied by a Mr David Parkinson, who had a senior and well paid job in hospital administration, which allowed him to stay at the guest house during the week, rather than commute from his home in Derbyshire, and go home to his wife and children at weekends, which was where he was now. A photograph of him and his family on the dressing table, showed him to be tall, late thirties early forties, with a *Clark Gable if he wasn't as good looking, look about him,* according to Alice, when they discussed the events of the day, later on that evening.

A brief look into the second floor bathroom, more out of courtesy than the need to know anything, showed it to be, as Philip had mentioned, identical to its upstairs neighbour, and with the second floor seen, they made their way downstairs.

On the first floor things were slightly different. This was the only floor to have had structural changes, with the former family room during the Victorian and Edwardian eras, partitioned, to form a new bathroom, and guest room. The two new rooms, separated by a small storage room, used by the staff for the storage of cleaning equipment and supplies. The placement of the storage room had the added bonus of saving the blushes of whoever was using the toilet and the ears of the guest in room three. The partition walls, being thinner than the originals

His knowledge of hospital wards and the indignity of using a commode behind a curtain, had been a factor in Doctor Howarth's design for the conversion. Such a considerate man was the doctor. Many people said it..

As, they entered the bathroom, neither woman was surprised to see it was almost identical to the other bathrooms, if somewhat smaller, Flo thought it cosy. Despite the fact that it was summer, and the bathrooms all had radiators, the size of the original bathrooms, made them seem cold and echoey, this one had a warmth about it.

She suddenly realised that Philip was talking and said "come again luv? I was miles away. Int this bathroom lovely Alice?" Alice nodded in agreement, as yet, she'd found nothing to moan about, but it wasn't even tea-time yet.

"I was saying, and father wouldn't mind me telling you this, that the investment of an additional bathroom has been returned more than threefold by the rents gained from the extra guest room. Shall we have a look at room three?"

"Flo had absolutely no idea what he'd just said about investments, and threefolds, so she just nodded like she understood perfectly. Alice being more money orientated replied, in her 'posh' voice, the one that got on Flo's nerves,

"Aim considering having hay new barthroom put in mayself. You must tell me when one purchased one's fittings. Ai've got more bedrooms than ai need"

Flo's response was a snort of derision, before saying, "you've got *three* and one of them was chopped in half, to put your toilet in. Pay no attention to her, Philip" Flo said to the grinning young man. It was a long time since he'd been in the company of his lovely down to earth, Flo, and he was remembering how happy he was when she was around. A lot more often than his parents were really, but, *they* were good sorts too, just busy, father, with his practice, mother, with her committees and charities. They'd given him the next best thing in Flo.

"I'll sort out the company's details for you" he said to Alice with a smile, and to Flo he gave a wink, then repeated his earlier offer "so, shall we look at room three?" and without waiting for an answer, he led the way, tapped briefly on the door, and unlocked it.

Room three, rented for the past three months to a medical supplies salesman, a Mr Harold Poole, was smaller than they'd expected, especially after the generous proportions of the other rooms, even the attic room could be described as 'roomy' in comparison. This room contained a single bed, small wardrobe and a slim chest of drawers. An easy chair and side table positioned to be shared between bed and chair, completed the furnishings, leaving just enough room to negotiate your way around *'As long as you're not ten ton Tessie'* thought Flo knowing Alice would be thinking something similar, and hoping she didn't open her gob and actually say it. She shot her a warning look but, Alice was too busy looking at the top of the wardrobe.

"Not very trusting is he?" she said pointing out the four suitcases atop the wardrobe, all with padlocks attached.

"When you're in the guest house business" replied Philip "You get to know that people have their eccentricities. We had one guest a couple of years ago, who put a hair across his door before going out in the evening, to see if any one was going in his room. A very strange chap he was"

"Sounds like a bit of a nutter" replied Flo, staring at Alice, who blushed, and hurriedly changed the subject,

"Them sinking ships give me the heebie-jeebies" she said,

with a shudder, referring to the room's obvious naval theme. Flo, had to agree, the Shipwreck surrounded by dead bodies in particular gave her the shivers, but, she liked the big steering wheel on the partition wall. All in all, the room was very agreeable, if small. No photographs, so they'd have to wait til later to see what Mr Poole looked like. The window overlooked the washing lines, but was still a pleasant view, as they left the room, Alice 'dropped' her hanky, bending down to pick it up she noticed two more suitcases under the bed, both padlocked like their companions, and she had one of her 'feelings'

'There's summat not right about him'

The final two rooms to be seen, were rooms one and two, inhabited by Misses Tippit and Barker respectively. Both these rooms although identical to the other front facing rooms, had the luxury of working fireplaces and were obviously inhabited by females. In room one, Miss Tippet's room, the theme of the wall art was floral arrangements. She was obviously a knitter as a part knitted cardigan, or Jumper was carefully spread over the side table next to copies of 'Lady' magazine.

"Just to forewarn you" said Philip, lowering his voice. *It wouldn't be the done thing to be overheard discussing guests* "Miss Tippit is a bit of a snob, and she can have a sharp tongue"

"Oh, she'll get on wonderfully well with Alice, then"

laughed Flo "do you *mind*!" retorted her friend with an offended tone, but, there was some truth in Flo's words, not that she'd ever admit it but, as soon as she'd seen the magazines and expensive toiletries, even the wool was expensive mohair, Alice had been impressed. At least they had one guest with a bit of class.

Miss Abigail Tippet, Philip explained, was personal secretary to a Consultant Surgeon with offices at the Infirmary and private consultation rooms on St John's street, the 'Harley street' of Manchester. In her mid to late forties and a spinster, like her neighbour and friend Miss Lucy Barker, unlike Miss Barker, she also had independent means, her bank balance regularly added to, by rental income on a row of shops in Cheetham Hill, bestowed on her upon the death of her parents, there being no son to inherit. A fact of which she was glad, she wasn't a people person and couldn't have envisaged life growing up with a sibling. She just about tolerated her best friend, as the ladies would come to find out.

In Miss Barker's room there was an air of clean untidiness, a little like Miss Barker herself, when they came to meet her, with her mismatching clothes and stray hairs that kept popping out of her bun. The theme is this room was fairies and sprites, and seemed well suited to the character shown by her bits and bobs. Her chair cushions hidden by a part crocheted doily, elaborately patterned to look like a spider's web. A battered and very old teddy bear given pride of place in the middle of her bed. Liz and Lily knew always to replace *Theodore* before leaving the room, Lily had once forgotten and Miss Barker had returned to find him perched on the dressing table, she'd been upset for days.

Like Miss Tippet, Miss Barker worked in a consultant's office, as a senior typist, at considerably less than Miss Tippit made. A circumstance that made Miss Tippit and others wonder how Miss Barker could afford the room. What they didn't know was, at ten years a resident, Miss Barker had initially rented room three. An occasion when she stepped into the breach, some four years after moving in, when all the staff except Liz had been snowed in one atrociously bad winter, and helped prepare meals and keep the guest house up to standard for the four days they couldn't get in had resulted in the doctor and his wife, offering her room two at the same price. She'd refused at first but, at the insistence of her landlords had reluctantly. But, eventually and gladly, moved in, where she was to meet her future best friend Miss Tippit, some two years later. Upon getting to know her better, and her style and taste in clothes, or rather lack of it, Miss Tippit presumed frugal living in all other areas, to be why she could afford it..

As the trio left Miss Barkers room Philip said "and that's it ladies. A lot to take in, I know, but, I've every faith in you" His last remark directed at Flo. "Look at the time" he exclaimed, "dinner will be served shortly, Beryl will bring yours to you in your rooms. I suggest we call it a day for now, I'm sure you must be exhausted. Now, don't worry about anything to do with work, for the rest of the evening, it's all in hand, it's Saturday tomorrow, we have only have three guests in residence over the weekend so, meals will be easy. If you'll meet me in the office tomorrow morning at seven, we'll get to work" he smiled at the women and stretched out an arm in the direction of the staff quarters.

"I won't argue with you" said a weary looking Flo "I'm shattered" and with that, she tapped Alice's arm and said "come on, we'll see you in the morning Philip luv"

As they trotted down the corridor Alice nudged her and said. "there's summat not right about him in room three, all them padlocks, what's he hiding?"

"Your commonsense" quipped Flo "'cos it's a mystery to me, where you keep it. Remember it's a guest house not a 'guessed' house" she smiled at her word play.

"You've just said the same word twice" scoffed Alice

"Oh shut up I'm getting you a dictionary for Christmas…If you live that long!"

"Yeah I might get murdered" and Alice tutted. *'we'll see who's right'* she thought. *'there's definitely summat not normal going on in room three'*

CHAPTER 8

As Flo closed the door to their quarters behind them., she let out a deep sigh and said "before I do another thing I need a brew and a cig, thank God I don't have to make the tea an' all. I never knew walking about could be so tiring"

"We weren't just walking though" replied Alice sympathetically "we had all that stuff to take in too, I'm still not to sure who's who and what's where"

"We'll be as right as rain in a couple of days" replied Flo heading for the kitchen area "now, how does this thing work?" A red light on the two ring burner, told her she'd turned something on, she filled the kettle and placed it on the ring. A slight hissing noise a couple of minutes later told her she done everything correctly.

With a full pot of tea, some biscuits -*Beryl would be round with their tea in about half an hour, but both women were starving and needed something to bridge the gap*- they sat at the kitchen table and both sat silently for a few minutes, sipping tea and nibbling on Peek Freans assortment

Alice broke the silence

"I'm still not happy about my bedroom"

"There's nowt wrong with it" replied Flo, trying not to smirk "it's"- *she searched for the right word* -"it's cosy"

"I'll die of suffocation ,I've seen bigger coffins"

"Open a window" Alice tutted and took a sip of her brew, "you can't swing a cat in there"

"Have you bloody brought one with you?" snapped Flo before saying more kindly, "oh come on, it's not that bad, the bed looks dead cosy and those are good quality pillows, have a feel when you're getting your nightie on. And you've got a chest of drawers for your clothes and a wardrobe, what more could you want?"

"Sufficient space between all them things, would do, if I breathe out walking past them, I'll get stuck. Like you do in sinking sand but with furniture"

"You don't *half* exaggerate"

"I'll fall out if I burp" said Alice, with a defiant look that said. *for everything you say, I've got an a comeback, missus!*

"Oh shurrup, you'll be so knackered when you finish for the day, you won't care that you cant waltz in it" she was interrupted by a knock on the door and a shocked looking Alice, said "Who's *that*?"

"Someone who works here obviously" mumbled Flo, more loudly she said, "Who were *you* expecting? Jack the Ripper?" She got up and answered the door, because it

didn't look like Alice was going to shift herself.

As expected, by Flo at least, it was Beryl with their evening meal on a tray.

"Come on in luv" she said with a smile.

Beryl had already worked out that Flo was the friendlier of the two. The other one, put Beryl in mind of her Mam's friend Enid. *A right cow if ever there was one!*

Shyly she explained that this was the usual routine for the housekeepers, a perk for the unsocial hours. It wouldn't do ,if in the middle of a long working day, Mrs Basker had to cook her husband's tea. Their day didn't officially end til ten o clock when the front door was locked for the evening. The doctor knew that good staff stayed when you treated them well.

Beryl went on to say that the pots would be washed and returned to the kitchen by the housekeeper, when she went to make the resident's supper, the kitchen staff having left as soon as the dinner pots were washed and put away.

"What is it" said Alice, a tad rudely, lifting the cloth that covered the tray.

"Erm, it's fish, we always serve fish of a Friday" Flo lifted the plates, covering the food and saw a good piece of cod with mashed potatoes and peas, parsley sauce in a jug to be poured according to taste, stood next to the plates, as did a plate of bread and butter "looks lovely" she said with a smile directed at Beryl.

"I'd have preferred kippers" said Alice sulkily

"We have kippers every second Friday" responded a nervous Beryl. "there's spotted dick and custard for afters" she said, as if offering compensation

"I'm not a custard person" sighed Alice, she'd firmly decided to be not pleased about anything.

"Have you *heard* you? Lady Muck" said Flo with a scoff in her voice, "if you was at home you'd be having sardines on toast or a chippy, or mooching round mine to see what I'd cooked. So, you can stop that whinging or I'll tell Beryl to serve you tapioca at every pudding"

"I hate tapioca" said an indignant Alice

"I *know!* ignore her, luv" an amused Flo said to Beryl, with a wink, Beryl knew she was gonna like Flo

"We have tapioca every second Tuesday, which is coming up this coming Tuesday. I'll tell Aunty Maureen to do you some peaches, we always do tinned peaches when someone doesn't like their dinner"

"So, if I don't want want lamb chops on the third Wednesday after the second Monday" said Alice sarcastically, "you'll put peaches on me mash, with gravy, will ya?"

Beryl giggled, Alice's sarcasm going over her head "no! you'd get extra veg"

Flo, addressing, Beryl, said "tell your Aunty Maureen that this looks lovely and we're both dying to get stuck in. Will we see you all before you both go?"

"We usually say our goodbyes around this time, once we've tidied up, me and Auntie Mo have to get off quick so we don't miss our bus, otherwise it's an 'alf an hour' wait at this time, and me Mam and Dad start to think we've been murdered, you'll hear us go though, cos you can hear the back door going from here"

"I've got it written down somewhere" said Flo, looking around for the envelope "but, just remind me, *what* time are you back in tomorrow?"

"We come in at two and finish at eight 'cept Saturdays when we come in at eleven and finish at six. We do the big kitchen clean on Saturdays too cos there's hardly anyone here, and we peel the spuds and everything for Sunday dinner, and -

Flo interrupted, thinking *'she'll never shut up if I don't'* "Aw, Beryl thanks luv, you'd better get a move on, you don't want to miss the bus"

"You're right" she giggled, she always spoke nineteen to the dozen, when she was nervous. As she turned to leave she said, "Liz asked me to remind you about the no flushing rule after ten"

"Oh don't worry, we won't forget. Philip flushed one for us earlier. Me ears are still ringing"

Beryl giggled again, and said "ours is an outside one at home, these one's here scare me a bit. I only go for number one's though" She lowered her voice to a whipser, "I can only do number two's at home" to which Alice made a retching sound and Flo gave her dig in the ribs, before opening the door to prompt Beryl to go "we'll see you tomorrow then luv" and with a bit of a curtesy, although, she didn't know why she did it, Beryl took her leave.

"Keep her well away from me" said Alice, you know I'm allergic to idiots

"I don't know how you're not forever sneezing then"

"What's that supposed to mean?"

"If you weren't an idiot, you'd know"

Used to her friends witticisms, Alice said nothing. She was too hungry to argue, and whether she preferred kippers or not, the food before them, did look tasty. They both sat in silence and ate a hearty meal, afterwards Flo washed and Alice dried. After a fresh pot of tea had been made and poured, both women sank into the two armchairs.

Alice had just picked up a magazine from the rack at the side of her chair, presumably Mrs Basker's chair and Flo was staring over at the telly looking for the *on* switch when the door knocked again."come on in Philip" Flo shouted cheerily as his head popped round the door and he said, "I've just come to say goodnight, and see if you need anything"

"We're fine luv" replied Flo, Alice nodded in agreement "Oh, if you could just explain how the telly works"

"Of course. It's the knob here, turn clockwise, it takes about five minutes to warm up" and with that, he said a final goodnight and left. "So, are you putting your *precious* telly on?" asked Alice, seeing Flo hadn't moved from her chair "you know what?" a tired looking Flo, replied "I'm to tired to even watch it, I'm gonna finish this cuppa and put me head down. I wonder how Bob and Joyce are getting on?" it had been such a hectic day, this was the first chance she had to think of them "I hope she did the kippers for tea"

Alice said nothing but she thought to herself *'I hope she can actually cook. I've never seen her anywhere near that cooker, the spoilt brat'*

"I'm sure they'll be fine" she finally said, stifling a yawn herself"

"Aw, it's been lovely to see Philip again" said Flo, changing the subject "He was only a nipper when I first came to Manchester"

"I remember him being born" said Alice, in her usual

show of one-upmanship. Flo ignored her. "I never liked him as a child" she continued "he came across as sly"

"Aw, bless, that was 'cos he had a squint, but it's gone now, and he's grown to a handsome young man. I wonder why he's not married?"

"He might be funny that way? he does have a high voice"

"He has a soft and kind voice you horrible woman"

Alice shrugged "Well, if *he's* not, the two old biddies on the first floor are *definitely* that way inclined"

"What do you mean old biddies? they're not much older than us, and *we* always go round together, no one says we're funny peculiar"

"That's 'cos we've both been married, we've got nowt to prove, you can tell we're normal"

"I'm not bloody sure about *you.* anyway, we haven't even met them yet"

"Time will tell...he's a weirdo an' all, the man in room three, I got the shivers in his room"

"You're making *that* up"

"I'm telling you there's summat not right about him,. there could be all sorts in them suitcases"

"Yeah, they could be full of LUGGAGE!"

"Time will tell" said Alice again, smugly

"Well, *she* looks a lovely young girl, Sally from the al -
attic room, oops I nearly said alley then" both women
giggled and then, Alice replied, unsurprisingly negative,

"I'm sorry Flo, but there's summat not normal about her
either. Did you see her clothes when I opened the
wardrobe? All long and dark. so, very last century, I've
seen nuns expose more flesh"

"She's very pretty though. imagine her in the right outfit,
she'd be a wow. From her photo, she puts me in mind of
a blonde Deanna Durbin"

"She puts me in mind of a nutter" sniffed Alice "mind
you, she might be hideously disfigured under there" Flo
sighed and didn't even bother arguing with her, she was
getting tired "we've still got the others to meet an' all, on
Monday" she said wearily,

"If this lot are anything to go by I'm expecting a traveling
freak show" replied her friend "I'm sure they'll be equally
impressed by you" snapped Flo "I'm going to bed. It's
gonna be a long first day, and summat tells me you're
gonna make it feel longer" she stood up and took her cup
to the sink.

"I can always go home" threatened Alice very
unconvincingly "See ya" said Flo blithely, and at that
moment she meant it, she knew she could manage, she'd
'kept house' for a family of six before now, with just a

cook to give a hand. They'd cried when she left, their loss being the doctor's gain.

Fearing she meant it, Alice changed her tune hastily, "Aw, you know I wouldn't leave me best mate in the lurch. I'm feeling tired meself, so, I'll say goodnight"

"Goodnight luv" replied Flo, and she waited until Alice had turned the 'big light' on in her room, before she switched the living room light off, and headed for her first night in a strange bedroom, and a strange bed.

Through the adjoining wall, she could hear Alice banging into stuff and saying "Ow!"

'She's doing it deliberately' thought Flo and sighed as she turned off the lamp and settled down, in bed, *'yep its gonna be a long day tomorrow.'*

The bed, comfier than her and Bob's if truth be told, began to work its magic. "*If you're not on your feet you're on your back" her auntie May -related by the fact she lived next door, not through any blood link - had said, "always invest in good shoes and a good mattress"* this *was* a good mattress, and she was asleep in minutes, her last conscious thought being *"if she doesn't shut up that ow-ing I'm gonna get up and slap her round the chops!"*

In her room, Alice sat on the bed occasionally slapping the wardrobe and shouting "ow!" *'She'll swap rooms in a couple of days if I keep it up',* she thought, with a smirk on her face. The bed *was* small in comparison to her own, but like Flo's, extremely comfy, the sheets smelled of freshly cut grass, and the pillows were like clouds, Alice too, was soon asleep.

Tomorrow was to be an eyeopening day for at least, one of them. .

CHAPTER 9

The next morning, as agreed, the ladies headed to the office at seven o clock, to meet Philip, for breakfast and a run down of the day. They found toasted crumpets, a dish of butter and pots of orange marmalade and raspberry jam waiting for them, as well as a pot of tea. Philip explained that breakfast was always a quick affair for the live-in staff, but mid-morning, they had a late 'full breakfast' using the left overs from the residents breakfasts, he noticed that Alice pulled a face when he mentioned leftovers and smiling, he said "I don't mean toast with a bite out of it, there's usually enough for a bacon and egg sandwich apiece, and it stays nice and warm in the serving trays" Alice shrugged and said "we'll see. I'm a bit funny about food that's been touched by other people"

"They're not diving into the sausages with their bare hands" scoffed Flo "did you not notice the serving tongs?" she tutted and turned her attention to Philip. "She doesn't think there's anything 'funny' about touching my leftovers, she's *forever* leaving mine, with a plate of summat in her hands" she rolled her eyes and Philip laughed. Alice decided to ignore her, but sipped her tea in the way, only she could, with an air of being offended.

By now, it was half past seven, and Philip suggested he

99

and Flo make their way to the kitchen to prepare breakfast for the four in situ guests, whilst Alice conducted the flushing of the toilets

"Why me?"

"Well" said Philip *"that* is Mr Basker's task while Mrs Basker makes a start on the breakfast"

"I'll tell you what we'll do" said Flo, with no intention of sticking to what she said, but knowing Alice needed placating "we'll take turns. Tomorrow you cook, and I flush"

"S'pose" said her friend, sulkily "so, let me get this straight" she said looking at Philip "all I do is flush?"

"All you do is flush" assured Philip

"*No* way, am I, bleaching toilets"

"He's already said that all you have to do, is flush" snapped Flo, so, get flushing! And look on the bright side, you're about to wake the world and his wife up. Why should *they* sleep when we're up?" she winked at Philip who understood her tactics perfectly. Alice's face broke into a sly grin "so, it's just them three toilets?"

"Just them three" Philip reassured her

"See you in a few minutes then" and she headed up the stairs. Flo and Philip grinned and made their way to the kitchen, they'd just reached the food preparation area when they heard the first rumble of pipework. "it serves as a wake up call too" laughed Philip, "we do have a gong but there's no need at breakfast. Now, are you ready for your first breakfast service at Oakenelm, Flo?"

"As ready as I'll ever be, pinny's on, hands are clean, let's get on with it, lad"

As they worked together to get the breakfast ready, Flo was impressed at the routine. The posh refrigerator, miles bigger than any she'd ever seen before, except on American films, held on it's middle shelf, all the ingredients needed to prepare a hearty cooked breakfast, the grill on the cooking range, able to toast eight pieces of bread at a time, and with only four guests to cook for, breakfast was well under control by the time Alice rejoined them.

"I'd have been here quicker" she said as she approached the prep area "but I got lost"

"How do you get lost coming down a flight of stairs?" mocked Flo

"Not on the stairs! I'm not an idiot. In the corridor, I turned left instead of right, and ended up back in the dining room, which got me thinking"

"Well, you carry on thinking luv" interjected her friend "and while you're doing it, start loading these trays onto that trolley"

Alice rolled her eyes, then rolled her sleeves up. When she had to be, she was a grafter. As she carted trays from table to trolley she looked at Philip and asked "What's that door for?"

"Which door?" he replied, "we have several"

"The one that's not a door anymore. The one that's been painted over to look like a bit of wall?"

"Oh, that one. When the house was in it's original state, that door led to a flight of stairs which brought the servants to a door, leading to what was the family room on the first floor, and is now room three and the bathroom. We blocked it up because there was need for it"

"So, where's the door to what was the family room?" Alice continued, her nosiness piqued. "Ah, it's locked and has had the door knob removed, same as the downstairs one. You can't see it because the wardrobe in room three is in front of it" he looked at his watch "Time to serve breakfast ladies. Are we ready"

"Ready, willing and able" responded Flo, she was enjoying herself, she loved being busy, loved being *'in service'* and ignored the look on Alice's face, she knew she was still thinking about the door. *'that nosy cow's gonna try and get in there'* she thought to herself. *'I'll be having a word later'* "Come on Alice" she said, jerking her friend out of her wandering mind "we're not here to relax, come on let's go"

After checking the trolley was laden with everything needed, Philip led the way to the dining room. As they passed the door that was no longer a door, in the corridor, Alice nudged her and raised an eyebrow knowingly, Flo nudged her back and nearly sent her flying

"Oy! what are you pushing me for?" said a sulky Alice"

"Sorry" said Flo, her voice dripping with insincerity "I tripped"

They entered the dining room and began setting out breakfast. Philip unlocked the back doors as was the usual procedure, Flo made a mental note to remember that. It'd been a lovely few days, how nice for the guests to be able to take their morning cup of tea on the patio. On sunny days she liked to sit in her back yard with a brew and listen to the birds, and the neighbours arguing. No neighbours were close enough to overhear here, but, it was a much nicer space to sit, than her back step.

A quick glance into the residents lounge told them that no one was downstairs, but footsteps and general murmuring could be heard, and soon the first guests appeared. "good morning Miss Tippet, good morning Miss Barker" said Philip cheerily as the first two guests took their seats at table one. "may I introduce you to our temporary managers? This is Mrs Holden"

"Call me Flo" she interjected, giving a quick bob of

welcome. "I've known this lad since he was knee high to a grasshopper, used to work for his Dad"

"Oh really?" said Miss Barker, the smile in her voice, matching the one on her face. He *has* mentioned you a few times" she said, referring to the doctor. Flo beamed with pride. "said you were a wonderful housekeeper" she continued. "thanks for stepping into the breach. Such a shame about Mr and Mrs Basker. We're going to go and visit them soon, aren't we Abigail?" She looked at her breakfast companion and waited for an answer

"If we have the time" was the grumpy response. She then turned her attention to Philip and gave her beverage request, leaving Lucy Barker, feeling a tad embarrassed. Her friend could be very brusque, and very snobby, she knew she be told off later for being too friendly with the 'help' But Lucy didn't judge a person on what they were, she went on feelings, and had taken to Flo immediately.

When Abigail was being particularly snobbish, a quite often occurrence, Lucy Basker was sometimes tempted to share her own secret, but never did. No one knew her secret, and never would. She liked the person she had become, no one ever needed to know where she'd really come from.

"We're off to to the Lake District for the weekend" she heard her friend saying to Philip, "so we need to finish breakfast as soon as possible, I want you to order a taxi to the station for ten?"

"Of course" replied Philip "And just to complete the introductions, this is Mrs Clough who will be assisting Flo"

"Call *me* Mrs Clough" interjected Alice, with a grumpy voice equal to that of Miss Tippet, who had already headed to the serving area to choose her breakfast, whilst Flo attended to their drink orders. A pot of tea for two.

Soon the other two guests appeared. Sally Henderson who looked exactly like her photograph, and was dressed in a long grey dress more suited to autumn than the lovely summer's day they were having. *'she's probably one of those who always expects it to rain'* mused Flo. *'what's she bloody hiding under there?'* thought Alice. Sally shyly nodded as the introductions were made by a slightly flushed Philip, but, noted Flo, she seemed oblivious to his obvious attraction. *'let's see what we can do about that,* she thought to herself, as she served Miss Henderson her requested tea, no sugar, just a drop of milk, a sudden grab of her arm by Alice, *who needed to cut her bloody fingernails,* alerted Flo to the appearance of Mr Harold Poole, and if truth be told, he did look slightly odd.

The bushiest eyebrows she'd ever seen, beneath a perfectly barbered short back and sides, had her wondering why he didn't ask the barber to take a couple of inches of the brows. Average height, with slim build and classic if old fashioned taste in menswear; suit, and tie, he gruffly said good morning in response to Philip's introductions and asked for a single cup of tea, no milk no sugar. As it was served he asked Philip if the papers had arrived. "bright and early this morning" responded Philip assuring him that, as usual they'd be placed on the table, in the reception area. Mr Poole picked up his cup of tea and headed there. Seeing that all the guests had been attended to, Philip silently caught the attention of Flo and Alice, and gestured towards the office where they took their places at the table

"Well, how did you find your first breakfast serving?" he enquired of Flo

"Nowt to it luv" was her welcome response. "we'll be as right as rain by Monday"

A slightly relieved Philip believed her, he could concentrate on Father's building work now, without worrying about Oakenelm "and *you* Alice?, he enquired more out of politeness than concern.

"Easy as pie" she responded "So what's next?" interjected Flo, and Philip looked at his watch, "Mrs Basker would usually check the to-do book about this time" he replied, pointing to a large bounded note book on the desk "to see if there's any little jobs needing Mr Basker's attention. A squeaky door, or loose fittings" Seeing Alice blanch he added "but, that's all in hand, whilst you are here, me and Fred will handle any little jobs, no need to be getting a tool box out Alice"

"I never had any intention" she sniffed "and I'd be

getting the first bus home if I was expected to do man's stuff. It's not natural"

Both Philip and Flo smiled at each other before Philip continued, "they should be done and dusted by now, we'll clear away, ready for Beryl to wash up, do a brief tidy up, spilled milk and anything like that, before her and Liz do the proper clean, and then you've got the morning to yourselves. Only Mr Poole is remaining at home today"

Alice shuddered *'it would be the weirdo'* she thought.

"Well, if you don't mind" replied Flo, "we'd like to assist the ladies with the cleaning, to get a feel for the place. You never know, the buses might go on strike or another world war starts and no one can get in"

"Good point" replied Philip with a smile, "but, have your proper breakfast first. Just help yourself to whatever's left over, the others will polish off the rest. I'm going to make a start on some little jobs, I'll be in Fred's shed if you need me, and I'll get Liz or Lily to knock on when they're ready to start the housekeeping" He stood up and headed back to the dining room, where with Flo and Alice's help, the trolley was laden with the remaining food and dirty pots, The tables were wiped and chairs put back in place, to give a semblance of tidiness, before the big clean.

As Flo and Alice sat down in their rooms to a banquet of still warm bacon, sausages, tomatoes and toast, with a fresh pot of tea, they mused over the events of the morning,

"Well the toilet flushing wasn't as bad as I thought it'd be" said Alice, munching on her toast, "no number two's"

"Do you mind!" replied Flo "I'm bloody eating!"

"What do you think of the guests?" she asked, ignoring Flo's chastisement

"They seem like nice people" replied Flo "what do *you* think?" and immediately regretted it as her friend seized on the opportunity to make her opinion and prejudices known.

"That Miss Tippet thinks she's the queen of bloody Sheba. She wants to sort out the wart on her neck before she looks down on other people, and the other one's a mouse, looks like one an' all. I wanted to give her a bit of cheese to nibble on. That young girl is not normal, did you see how she was dressed on such a lovely day? I bet she's hideously disfigured under all that clothing, and as for him in room three, he's got more hair on them eyebrows than the lot of our heads put together. He's shifty"

"It's what a person *is*, not what they look like, you moaning cow" retorted Flo "is there no-one you like or trust?"

"Yeah meself"

A knock on the door saved Flo from having to reply "Come in" she called and a smiling Lily stood in the doorway

"Liz said to tell you we're gonna make a start on the guest rooms, she'll meet you by the storage room on the first floor, whenever you're ready, we've already done the dining room and reception"

"What about the lounge?" enquired Flo.

"At weekend we do that room last, Miss Henderson's still in there at the moment, but the others have gone out"

"Well, we'll just wash these pots and meet you up there in about five minutes"

"Okay" and with that a smiling Lily turned and headed back to the main kitchen. In the small kitchenette Flo took charge. "I'll wash you dry" she instructed Alice, and both ladies did their bit to clean up the breakfast pots. With a quick hello to Maureen and Beryl who were deep cleaning the oven as they passed through the kitchen, Flo and Alice made their way to the first floor store room.

Their first day on the job was about to begin in earnest and it was to be an eye opener in more ways than one, especially for Alice.

CHAPTER 10

The storage room was surprisingly roomy, and very well stocked. Ceiling to floor shelving on the left hand side, held all the linen necessary for bed changing, a pile of white fluffy towels and dark green eiderdowns, obviously for the winter changeover completed the stock. Flo peered around looking for the winter curtains. Liz seemed to read her mind and said "the winter curtains are massive, we keep them in the big cupboard at the back of the office" Flo smiled and nodded, this girl has sense, she thought.

To the right was more shelving, containing cleaning products, mop heads and cloths. Alice thought she'd never seen so much Vim in her life, even the local shop didn't have that much scouring powder. Flo enquired as to the routine they followed and Liz told her that they had a basket each for cleaning materials and cloths which they filled here and carried between floors, she pointed out a large basket on wheels in the corner, on bed change days, the dirty linen would be chucked in and Mr Basker would carry it down the stairs and cart it over to the laundry room, where Mrs Basker would load the washing machine, and hang out the washing to dry on fine days, or use the indoor maidens situated around the laundry room in rainy weather, an oil fire was usually lit to aid drying. There was a laundry service for the residents if required, those that went home at weekends usually took their dirty washing with them, but, regular requests were received from the ladies on the first floor. Alice was relieved to know that Fred would lug the laundry basket down the flight of stairs, and quite excited that she and Flo would get to use a modern washing machine. Bed change days were Wednesdays and Saturdays, the big wash day was Tuesday and any residents laundering requests were fitted in between.

The resident request book which lodged under the counter of reception, would be updated with guest requests and checked by Liz each morning. Today Mr Poole had said he didn't need his room attending to nor bedding changed, and room seven was already made up in anticipation of its new guest, so linen for six rooms was selected, the two for the floor they were on, put to one side, and the other four sets divided between Liz and Lily, with a basket on each arm, they refused offers of help from Flo *"You need to see what we do, in case you ever need to do it"* they led the way upstairs, as they passed the second floor, Liz opened the door to room five with her master key and left the bedding for that floor on the arm of the chair, then they made their way to the top floor, Lily heading for the attic room with Flo accompanying her and Alice following Liz into Mr Hawkins room.

As expected, the attic room was immaculate, with the bedding already removed and folded neatly on the armchair. Lily told Flo the story of young Sally's neatness and invited her to admire the view, as she did, and whilst getting her breath back, a cursory polish and check of the waste bin, was completed by Lily as per her routine, they then headed for the next room to be done, which today was none, so she pulled out a canvas bag from her basket and popped the dirty washing in, letting Flo know that Liz had an identical bag for her laundry.

Their next port of call, was the bathroom, where Lily proceeded to wash and clean the bath and sink, remove any dirty towels and replenish with fresh ones from the cupboard. Liz and Alice joined them just as Lily was doing the last job, the cleaning of the toilet bowl and Liz explained that it was the housekeepers job to check and replenish supplies in the bathrooms. This was usually done on a Sunday, as like Flo and Alice, neither the housekeeper nor her husband, were regular churchgoers so, they had the time before finishing for the rest of the day. Flo was impressed at how well the staff worked together, Alice was dizzy with it all.

"I'm not sure I can remember all this"

"You won't have to" said Flo "I'm here" and she grinned whilst Alice pulled a face

The other two floors were done to the same routine, Liz pointing out that once the bed changing was completed. Lily would go back upstairs to mop and sweep all floors, whilst she tackled the lounge with the help of Beryl if needed, the final area for her and lily being reception and the office, before break time.

In no time at all, thanks to the hard work and dedication of the staff, the comfort of the guests was ensured and the ladies headed to the kitchen where Maureen had just finished washing down the cooking range. She informed Flo that Philip was in the office and had said to pop in after lunch, which Beryl who had suddenly appeared from the corridor, informed them was waiting in their rooms. Flo's response, much to Alice's disgust was "from Monday can we have our breaks with you? It's different for the regular housekeepers, they live here but we'll pick things up quicker if we spend time with you lot, won't we Alice?"

"I could pick it up just as much if I was sat in a comfy chair in my own room," she mumbled, before saying more loudly "I'm not mithered," followed by a sigh that called her a liar. Another thing to have a '*word*' about later, thought Flo, and headed to their rooms without saying another word, just a roll of the eyes was all she needed to convey her disgust at her 'miserable' friend.

As they entered, both were delighted to see that Beryl had tidied up, not that they'd left a mess, but the air smelled of polish and bleach, nectar to Flo. On the table sat a huge plate of ham sandwiches with the crusts off, a plate of very posh looking cakes, a couple of Scotch eggs and two quarters of pork pie. Flo immediately put the kettle on, and they ate and drank without saying a word. Both

engrossed in early editions of the *Manchester Guardian.*
Flo broke the silence by saying "Aw, my Bob will be
sorting out the table for his pools results soon. I hope our
Joyce is feeding him properly"

Alice without looking up from her paper replied "I bet
that Joan is rooting through me drawers as we speak", Flo
tutted and went back to her newspaper.

A knock on the door, broke the blissful silence, it was
Beryl with a message from Philip to meet him in
reception whenever they were ready. After putting the
leftover cake and sandwiches to one side for supper, they
headed off to reception.

"So how are you finding it all?" he asked as he looked up
from the book he was browsing through, "we're fine,
stop fretting" replied Flo in mock anger. "Now give us
something to do, we've survived the first night, and let's
have it right we're not here on holiday are we, we need to
work, especially at the rate your parents are paying" Philip
smiled "in that case, would you mind if I went out for a
bit? I could do with popping into town before
everywhere shuts"

"You get off luv", said Flo, she was looking forward to
being left in charge, and relished the thought of some
time alone with the staff. "Now what's in that enormous
box, on the desk? Surely that isn't meant to be here?"

"Practical as ever Flo, and never wrong" said the young

man "did you hear that Alice, she said to her unusually quiet friend "Philip's got me spot on" She burst out laughing, Alice who really wanted to sit down and have a read as she usually did on a Saturday afternoon, retorted "you should hear yourself, you sound like old Mother Riley".

"And you look like her" came the reply, quick as a flash. "now then luv, carry on telling me about that box?" she said turning her attention back to Philip who replied "these are new supplies for the storeroom. If I take the box up would one of you kindly unpack it and put the stores away?"

"I'll do that" said Alice quickly, she loved having a root and it'd be nice to get some peace and quiet on her own.

"Are sure you'll be alright doing something on your own?" said Flo with a modicum of sarcasm "I'll be fine, at least I'll be somewhere bigger than my bedroom", replied Alice, with sarcastic emphasis on every word.

"It *is* a small room" interjected Philip trying to ease what he thought was tension between the two women, but, was as normal as breathing to them. He decided to change the subject completely. "Flo, I've left some books in the office I'd like you to go through them to familiarise yourself with the task ahead -Nothing to do with the accounts or anything like that" he said, noticing the look of terror on her face. Her Bob sorted out the bills and stuff at home, she could work wonders with her housekeeping, but Bob always saw to the big bills. "just the residents' request book, and our to-do book for the coming week" he continued "I'll be an hour or two, but we've only got one resident currently at home, and just the one expected back. It's steak pie and potatoes for dinner this evening, and as is our usual practice when the guest list is so minimal the evening meal will be served in their rooms, and once you've collected the dishes your job is done for the evening, and Saturday evening television is very good" he said, looking at Flo. "Right then!" he exclaimed, clasping his hands in front of him, and looking around "I'll get this box upstairs for you, Alice, and then I'll toodle-oo off out for a bit"

"I'll walk up with you" she said, eager to have a nosy. Flo turned and headed into the office, where two large books waited for her on the desk, she sat in the comfy chair, opened the first book, and began to read.

As they walked up the stairs, Alice asked "so, who's the guest who's stayed in?"

"Mr Poole" replied Philip, and Alice froze

"Everything ok?" asked Philip with concern, noticing the colour had drained from her face. Not wanting to share her theory that he had the eyebrows of a murderer, Alice began to walk up the stairs again and in her best, 'What *are* you talking about' tone replied "Of course I am...I got me foot stuck on the carpet, has the girl who cleans it forgot a sticky bit?"

A little offended at Alice's insult to a member of staff, Philip replied tersely "We're very happy with how each person does their job here. Ah! here we are," he took a key from his pocket and opened the door. At his request Alice turned on the light, and he set the box down on the floor, and with a penknife taken from his pocket carefully cut open the top of the box. Alice was eager to be left alone, her nosiness overtaking her fear of being murdered by pair of eyebrows.

"How do I lock the door when I'm finished?"

"Good question" Philip handed her his master key. "I do have one each for you and Flo" he said as he turned to go "I'll sort them out as soon as I return. they're in the safe" and with that, he left, to run his errands.

Alice was not sure if she liked the sound of living with a safe. In her favoured romantic novels, all the best people had a safe, housed behind an oil painting, but, with *'Rasputin'* in the house, the likelihood of her being 'murdered' increased if money was involved too. And what if he thought there were jewels as well? She was beginning to regret having just read *The Curse Of The Jeweled Tiara* in which every member of Crown Prince Rudolph's court had been hideously murdered after touching a tiara, sent to him by a despicable foreigner as a gift on the occasion of his marriage to a stunningly beautiful and virginal Duke's daughter, only for her, too, to fall prey to the murderer, he would end up defeating the murderer and marrying a milkmaid named Alicia.

Alice saw that as a sign. She contemplated running downstairs and getting Flo to come back up with her, but her eyes landed on the box and nosiness got the better of her. '*He's probably in the lounge anyway*', she thought, *especially if he's got a cat to swing.* She thought of her own room and tutted, before lifting the flap of the box to see what treasures lay within.

CHAPTER 11

It was indeed a treasure trove, that lay before her. Blocks of scented soap, new chamois, containers of cleaning products, tubs of wax polish. Alice, despite her permanent intention to be miserable everywhere she went, was enjoying herself. She liked sorting stuff out and stacking things neatly. She had almost contemplated buying a shop when her late husband's death insurance had come through, but, she'd figured it'd make him spin in his grave faster, if she just sat on her backside and squandered it on twin-sets from Kendals for a while, still, it wasn't too late, and she had a more than tidy lump sum remaining, along with the regular monthly payments from his wonderful life insurance policy *'I might consider investing in a guest house meself'* she mused *'watch Flo say I'm copying if I do that, well, I'll tell her straight! it's a free world, just cos she said she wants a guest house, dunt mean I can't have one'.* She happily stacked goods, and argued with people in her head, til her concentration was broken by a woman's voice. "Is that you Flo?" she called out, as she opened the door and looked around the landing. No one was there. She shrugged her shoulders and went back to her stacking. It was probably one of the other staff, titivating something or the other. She'd begrudgingly come to the conclusion that they were all good workers, even Beryl, the daft one. She carried on her sorting out, and then she heard the voice again. This time she didn't call out, she held her breath and listened. There it was again, she couldn't make out what was being said but it was definitely a woman's voice. She crept to the storage room door and using expertise, gained from many years practice, opened the door quietly. She was impressed and grateful that none of the doors squeaked. she adored a well oiled hinge, it saved so much embarrassment, people always got the wrong idea, when they caught you on the other side of their door. Strangely, the voice although still audible, had faded when she'd gone out into the corridor. She shrugged again, thinking *'It's probably the girls in the Kitchen, sound must travel funny in this house',* closed the door again and headed for the shelving at the back of the storage room. She pushed the current stock to one side to dust the shelf, before filling it with the contents of the box. That's when she heard the voice again. This time louder, and the realisation hit her, the *voice* was coming from behind the wall, and behind the wall was room three. Mr Eyebrow's room. He had a woman in his room! hastily she looked around for what she needed. There was a tin half full of soda crystals, so, she tipped them on to the shelf and held the empty container to the wall, with her left ear, *the one she considered her best ear for listening*, resting on it, sporadic words started to come through

"But why can't I go"- something unintelligible *"you promised"* Then a mans voice, definitely him *"Shut up, shut up"* then so loud that Alice jumped *"I SAID SHUT UP!"*

'I need to get Flo up here I knew there was summat not normal about him, and I've read the rulebook, no visitors of the opposite sex. You're getting evicted mate' she thought gleefully, she'd thought he was dodgy from the moment she'd seen them padlocked suitcases. *'He's a bleedin sex maniac. I bet he saw Philip go out and thought he could pull the wool over our eyes, well you've met your match mate'* She hurriedly tidied up, sweeping the soda crystals back into their tub, made a mental note to bring a glass up with her next time, and headed for the door, to report to Flo. With any luck they could have him out before the day was done. But, as she opened her door she heard another door open, it was *his,* she jumped back in the room and shut her door. *'I'm not scared'* she told herself *'but what if he grabs me knowing I've uncovered his secret.?..the pervert!* The sound of a door being locked and footsteps which sounded like just one person, *was he carrying her?* going down the stairs, told her it was safe to go out. She wondered what Flo's face would look like when she saw him swanning past with some tart. After peeping out to make sure the coast was clear, she locked the storage room door, remembering to take the empty box, and headed for reception to watch it kick off. Flo knew the rules too, she'd go mental that her beloved doctor's rules were being flouted

She found Flo, stood behind the desk "Well, what happened?" she asked

"Come again?" said Flo, with a confused look on her face.

121

"With *him*, from room three?"

"Oh, Mr Poole. Seems like a nice enough chap, said he's popping out to see friends and won't need dinner, but he'll be back before we lock up. Int this key cupboard lovely? Solid oak - And Just to remind you when you're on the desk, the residents have to leave their key when they go out"

It was Alice's turn to be confused "but, what about the woman?" she asked, with a frown of confusion.

"What woman?"

She started to shake with frustration and her voice got higher "the woman that was in his room with him. I heard them"

"You're hearing things, there was no woman with him. It's not allowed anyway, this is a respectable establishment, not a boudoir"

"You mean brothel"

"Well, you'd know!"

Still too confused to be offended by what Flo had just said, she said "Flo, as God is my witness, I heard a woman in his room, when I was sorting out the stock, and I heard it as clear as a bell"

"What was she saying?"

"I couldn't hear exactly, it was muffled but she said something about wanting to be let out"

"How is that 'as clear as a bell?' Flo scoffed "are you on the change? You're hearing things, and it could have been the radio"

"Did *you* see a radio in his room?"

"Not that I can recall, but I didn't see a woman either" Flo laughed

"That's it, laugh at me" said Alice getting angry "you won't be laughing when you're murdered in your bed, 'cos if he left here alone, she's still in his room, and God only knows what state she's in. I think we should check his room, and then call the Police"

"I think you should shut your gob" said Flo, with some menace in her voice. "we're not stood on your street watching the neighbours get evicted. I don't want Philip coming back and thinking we're fishwives"

"Do you want him coming back to a woman locked in a guest's room?"

Flo looked at her for a few moments, knowing she wouldn't let it go. She felt in her pocket for the master key Philip had given her before setting off on his errands and with a tut and a shake of her head said, "Come on then Miss Marple, show us where the body is"

The women headed up the stairs. Just as Flo was about to

unlock the door Alice said "Hang on. I need to prepare myself, we don't know what we're gonna see behind there"

She took several deep breaths to steady herself whilst a bemused Flo quipped "are you ready now Sherlock?" without waiting for an answer she unlocked the door. The room was empty. Flo smirked whilst Alice searched under the bed, opened the wardrobe and then stood with a perplexed look on her face. "but, there was a woman in here. I heard her voice"

Glancing round for a radio, but seeing no evidence of one, Flo said in a more kindly tone "You're not used to the house yet, the voice could have come from anywhere. I bet it was Beryl when she was taking the rubbish out, and Mr Poole probably had his window open"

"But, I was sure, it was coming from his room" came the confused reply. With no evidence to back up her claim, Alice began to think Flo was possibly right"

"C'mon" said Flo "We don't want him coming back unexpected and finding us rooting around in his room. It's nearly tea-time, Maureen's done a lovely steak pie. Miss Henderson's is on the hot plate til she comes in and Liz is here til eight so she'll serve her when she gets back. Lets go and have our tea and I'll tell you what we're doing tomorrow. The cook doesn't come in remember so, we're doing the Sunday dinner"

"Don't be putting me on spud peeling" said Alice

"We don't peel spuds" replied Flo in an indignant posh voice. "we're housekeepers, and Beryl peels 'em all the night before, in fact everything's prepared even the chicken's stuffed. All we've got to do is shove it in the oven"

"Chicken?" said Alice, with a smile on her face, "can I have a leg?"

"I'm sure we can come to some agreement" replied Flo, relieved her friend had 'forgotten' about the man in room three. "Let's go and have summat to eat. I don't know about you but my tummy thinks my throat's been cut"

"My throat's as dry as a bone. I'm gagging for a brew"

They both enjoyed their meal, Maureen made excellent pastry, and whilst on their second cup of tea, Philip knocked on to let them know he was back, and would lock up. With their duties done for the day, they both settled down for a night in front of the telly, before bidding each other goodnight and heading off to bed.

In their respective rooms, both went over the events of the day. Flo was really settling in now and couldn't wait for the challenge of running it alone. She flipped through a magazine, but tiredness overwhelmed her, and in minutes she was sound asleep.

Alice lay wide awake, the events of her day still muddled.

She accepted it could have been a voice coming from anywhere, but, it had seemed so real, seemed so close. She fell into a fitful sleep, and awoke in a cold sweat a couple of hours later, she was genuinely frightened, of what, she didn't know, but, there was definitely something not right about the man in room three. She got up and headed towards her friend's bedroom, where she slowly and quietly opened the door, startling herself a little as it creaked. She froze and listened. Silence except for the sound of steady breathing coming from the bed

She crept closer,

"Flo are you awake?" Flo did not reply, she merely turned over slightly and carried on her dream, involving Cary Grant and a sherry trifle. Alice leaned over and gently rocked her shoulder

"Flo" she whispered. No response. "Flo?" A little louder this time "FLO!",

Flo jumped up in mild panic. Unaware of where she was for a brief moment, then she saw Alice's face coming into focus, and she fumed

"WHAT?"

"You're awake" said Alice, with a smile.

Flo frowned and looked at Alice with eyes narrowing, she spoke with what Joyce called 'that threatening tone' in her voice "I bloody am now!"

"I can't sleep at all" replied Alice,seemingly oblivious to the anger in Flo's voice. In reality she was very aware, but found it easier to ignore it, Flo could never stay mad with her for long

Still sounding grumpy, Flo retorted "It's *not* a problem I was having" She plumped her pillows and turned onto her left side, leaving Alice to look at her back. Alice sighed, a sigh full of self pity. Flo sighed too, her sigh full of '*Why did I bring her?*' She turned to face her friend "Well, whats the bloody matter then? Why cant you sleep?"

Alice sat down on the edge of the bed "I cant get that girl out of me head"

"What girl?"

The one I heard in room three. Rasputin's room

"His name" said Flo indignantly "is Mr Poole"

"With them eyebrows, he puts me in mind of Rasputin" said Alice, dismissively "anyway it's the girl I'm talking about, not him, the murdering swine!"

'I'm getting nowhere with this idiot' thought Flo as she sat upright, and smoothed the blanket out, either side of her. She decided to change her tone, and opted for a patronising one. "Alice luv, we searched it not five minutes after he'd gone out, and found nothing. We both agreed, dint we? that there's no way she could have left

with him, without one of us seeing" She paused for a moment to see whether or not, her words were 'sinking in' Alice still looked perplexed, which was nowt new. Flo took Alice's hand and continued "and Philip was on the desk when he came back, *alone,* and he locked the front door as soon as he came in, dint he?" Alice, nodded in agreement."you must have imagined it Alice, its been an hectic few days, we've met loads of new people. Maybe you got confused?"

Alice took umbrage "Are you saying I'm senile? I'm barely forty"

"Does it matter ?" snapped Flo "and stop interrupting when I'm trying to explain things" She took a deep and calming breath, before continuing "like I said, there's a lot of people here, we've had to get to know a lot of new people in a short space of time. Do you agree, that you might have just thought you heard a woman in that room?" Alice hesitated, Flo continued "It might be down to lack of sleep *She was getting fed up now* why don't you try getting some!" she said in a sarcastic tone, and once again she lay down and turned her back on Alice

Silence for a few moments, then Alice replied, defiance in each word "I *did* hear a woman in his room"

Flo sat bolt upright "Okay, I believe you" she cried, more in a desperation and the need to sleep, than actual belief. "we'll talk about it in the morning, She let out a big yawn, and looked at the clock, it was a quarter to two "Have you seen the time?" she exclaimed "Its the middle of the night, we're up at six. Go to bed Alice" She flopped back down on her pillows

"Can I sleep with you?"

Knowing the consequences if she said no, Flo begrudgingly agreed "Alright then, just don't touch me with your feet, and don't talk to me!"

Alice grinned and got in. "Shove up then" she commanded Flo "if you don't want me to touch your feet, move 'em from my side" Flo said nothing, and shuffled over. Quietness came over the room...For a few seconds

"Flo?"

"WHAT?"

Alice tutted at Flo's tone "I just need you to know, I did *not* imagine it, I don't know where she went but she was most definitely in there" There was an adamant tone to her voice

"I've said I believe you" replied Flo, in a kinder tone "we'll sort it out in the morning, good night"

"I caught him staring at me before. What if he's got a thing for murdering women?"

"I wouldn't worry 'cos if you don't shut up and go to sleep I'm gonna murder you meself" There was definite menace in Flo's voice. Alice decided to keep quiet, and lay back in the bed,replaying what she'd heard in her head. *'There's no way that I imagined that'* she mused *'I heard her as plain as day. So where did she go?'*

The layout of the room,appeared in her head. Her eyes darted from side to side, as she did a search of the room in her mind's eye, and then it hit her! The one place they hadn't looked, was under the floorboards. She'd read of the clever hiding places used by Jews to hide from the Nazis during the War, there could be a room under the floorboards or a secret staircase. The notion came to her that this was possibly a daft idea, but she reminded herself, was it any dafter than a woman just disappearing into thin air? She briefly contemplated telling Flo her brilliant theory but, her deep steady breaths told Alice, she was already asleep. *'I'll tell her first thing'* thought Alice, and she lay back, thinking of how to move the rug. Nine tenths of the rug was covered by the bed only the legs of the headboard side stood on the wooden polished floor beneath. *'I'll get Flo to lift and I'll roll the carpet back'* Alice heard Flo's gentle snores and snuggled down in the bed, she was feeling sleepy now... *'It might be easier to lift the bed from the headboard side,which, given the limited space would mean a tight squeeze'*

'Thinking makes you really tired' she thought, as she burrowed further under the blankets. As she drifted off she thought she heard a voice saying "Oy! Stop touching me with your feet" but she ignored it as a wave of built up tiredness washed over her, and lulled her into restful

repose.

It was getting light by the time she fell into her own deep sleep, and she wasn't best pleased to be woken up, what seemed two minutes later, by an annoyingly cheery Flo. The happenings in room three, were the first thing that came to mind after she'd been awoken. Daft, she might be, mad she wasn't, She didn't hear voices ! She was determined to get to the bottom of Mr Poole's sordid secret. Whether Flo believed her or not.

CHAPTER 12

Sundays at Oakenelm were as lazy as a Sunday could get
when you have paying guests. With only Mr Poole and
Miss Henderson in residence, breakfast was served on
trays in their rooms, Philip having taken their orders the
previous evening. Flo now comfortable with using the
range, whipped up the full works for Mr Poole and a hard
boiled egg with toast for Miss Henderson whilst Alice
tidied up the housekeepers quarters. The staff had offered
to come in that day, but Flo had declined, she was a quick
learner and knew she could manage with Philip and Alice.
whilst Philip acted as waiter and delivered the breakfasts
at nine, she made a start on their own breakfast and all
three were soon sat down to a hearty meal at the kitchen
table.

No guest rooms were attended to on Sundays unless an
emergency occurred, and with free time on their hands,
Flo and Alice planned to have a walk round the grounds
after serving lunch, their only other responsibilities to the
guests being the the tea-time sandwiches, bread sliced by
Beryl, and ready to be buttered and pasted and cake
already plated up in the larder, and after that, the night
time cocoa.

Philip would be leaving shortly after lunch, so, he excused
himself and went to the office, to gather the paperwork
he needed and check tomorrow's to-do list to ensure Flo

had everything to hand for whatever occasion arose.

Both guests had requested their meals be served in their rooms, and Flo was happy to oblige as it meant the dining room wouldn't need a going over. Around eleven o clock, the twosome made their way to the kitchen to start cooking the meal prepared by Maureen. Potatoes and cabbage, peeled and chopped were waiting in their water filled pans, the chicken, stuffed and trussed, sat in the fridge in its roasting tin, ready to pop in the oven, all Flo needed to do was make the gravy. For afters Maureen had made a fruit salad and left a jug of cream.

"I wish every Sunday dinner I made was like this" Flo said as she shoved the chicken in the oven"

"You'd get sick of it after a few weeks" replied Alice "chicken's lovely but I wouldn't want it every Sunday"

"I didn't mean *what's* for dinner, I meant the fact it's all ready to pop in the oven and on the stove. It wouldn't mither me, if I never peeled another spud in my life"

With the Sunday lunch ready on the trays, and no sign of Philip, Flo took a tray and told Alice to get the other one, her eyes narrowed "I'm not taking *his* dinner. I might not come out alive, 'cos I was *not* hearing things, he had a woman in there, she's probably taking her last breath in one of them padlocked suitcases as we speak"

Flo rolled her eyes, at the sheer daftness of her friend "okay, I'll take his, and you take Miss Henderson's"

"She's all the way at the top! Three flights of stairs and another bit. Can't she come down for it?"

"It's a bloody guest house, not a workhouse, no, she can't! Now, make your choice, the risk of murder or getting out of breath?"

With a tut, Alice picked up his tray "you'd better wait with me, til he comes to the door"

"Course I will" said Flo, with no intention of waiting and she headed for the staircase with a grumpy Alice following behind. A quick shout of *'dinner's ready'* as they passed the office alerted Philip and he offered to deliver the trays. "no you're alright luv "said Flo, before Alice could hand him her tray "go and get your dinner, it's plated up and being kept warm in the oven. Yours is the plate at the front" she lowered her voice "I've given you a leg" Philip grinned, she hadn't forgotten his childhood favourites.

"I hope I've got a leg too" said Alice as she traipsed behind Flo "I did ask"

"You've got what you've been given. Now knock on with that tray"

"Wait for me then...where you going? I thought you was gonna wait for me?"

"I'm walking up slowly to keep the gravy warm. I can still see you, go on, KNOCK!"

As soon as Alice turned to knock, Flo sped up and was soon out of sight" The door opened a fraction and a curt voice said "*What?*" Alice held back the temptation to smash the tray in his face, as soon as he showed it. He might well be a murderer, but there was no need to be rude. "Your lunch is served" she said with gritted teeth, and his voice took on a kinder tone "just leave it outside the door, please. I'll get it in a minute" She wanted to chuck it at him, but, slowly bent and left the tray, and with that she headed back to the staff kitchen, to find Philip tucking into his meal, Flo joined them within moments

"Aw, she's a lovely girl that Sally, I told her to come and join us if she wants" Philip reddened, but Flo didn't notice and continued "oh, I know it's not the done thing to have a guest in the staff quarters but we could have all sat in the dining room, anyway, she's studying for something so she said no, but in a lovely way. Did you serve Mr Poole alright Alice"

"Yeah" came the terse reply. She'd have her words with Flo, later, when Philip had gone. Flo, grabbed a tea towel and pulled the plates containing her and Alice's food, from the oven. As Alice lifted the plate covering her meal, a look of disappointment spread across her face.

"What's up?" asked Flo, knowing full well what was up

"I asked for a leg"

"You've got one"

"It's a wing!"

"Same thing as a leg to a bird. Are you enjoying yours Philip?" she asked, noticing he was trying not to laugh, and she winked at him, "It's absolutely tip top Flo. I'd forgotten how delicious your gravy is"

"Family recipe" she replied smugly "the secrets in not using too much flour, and adding a knob of butter, but, beyond that me lips are sealed. Now tuck in everybody, we've got fruit salad and cream for afters"

"Have I got the same or do I get an apple an orange, and the use of a Cow?" asked a very sarcastic Alice, still fuming about her 'leg' "if it was trifle, would I get hundreds and thousands on mine or would I have to settle for tens and twenties?"

"Shurrup you moaning Minnie" was Flo's only response as she tucked into her own meal, and reminisced about tea times of the past with Philip.

With the meal finished and Philip collecting the used plates from the guests, it took the women no time at all to wash and tidy everything away.

It was now time for Philip to go back to his family home, until the weekend "Now are you sure, you're ready Flo? I can always leave early in the morning?" He was relieved when she told him not to be daft

After making sure she had his home telephone number, and reminding her to tell the girls not to bother with a bed change in his room as it didn't need it, the young man gathered his things and with a cheery goodbye, left through the back door. The sound of his car engine starting, then getting louder and fading, told them he was on his way.

"Come on then, grab a cardi Alice, and let's have a wander in the gardens"

"I'd better get me coat in case it rains"

"We're not going to *town*, we're sitting out in the garden. Would you put on a coat to go in your back yard"

"I would if it was the size of these grounds. Hang on, do you want yours?"

"Do I eck, just bring me cardi"

Alice returned, wearing her mac, and carrying Flo's cardi. As she shoved it on Flo said "we'll have a wander through the front gardens first, we've barely seen 'em since the day we arrived" As they headed to the door she sighed " Seems like ages ago, dunt it? I'm expecting to go home and find our Joyce married with kids"

"And where do you expect to find Bob?" smirked Alice, in her head she said *'his grave?*

"Are you bringing up his age again? 'cos don't make me start! are *you* jealous 'cos your husband couldn't even make it out of his twenties"

"*That* is cruel Flo"

"Pot, kettle, and bloody black!"

"Anyway, at least I had a husband in his twenties"

"You know what? I'm beginning to doubt that your Eddie had a tragic accident. I think he topped himself, so he wouldn't have to spend his thirties and forties with you, now, are you coming outside or are you just gonna stand there collecting flies?" Without waiting for an answer Flo stormed out of the front door. Alice left it a few minutes, so she could say she came out of her own accord, if it kicked off again and she found Flo sitting on one of the benches in front of a beautiful flower bed.. She sat down beside her, and for a few minutes neither one said a word. Alice broke the silence "I fancy a cig, have you got yours on you?"

"Is the Pope a catholic" Flo replied, reaching into her pinny and pulling out a pack of Woodbines and some matches.

"Have you not got tipped ones?"

"I'll repeat, *is* the Pope a *Catholic*? You're right, *no,* I haven't. I *never* have tipped ones, do you want one of these, or not?"

"Go on then" Flo passed her the box and carried on staring at the flower bed '*Obviously still sulking*' thought

Alice. "Are you having one too Flo?"

Flo turned slowly and said "Is the Pope...?" and both women cracked up laughing for a good minute.

"Sorry about that before, Flo"

"Me too" They sat together in silence again, both puffing on a cigarette whilst enjoying the fresh air and sunshine, until, this time Flo broke the silence, "Should we get rid of these dimps and have a wander round the back?"

"I'm game" came the reply. They headed to the rear grounds, stopping to throw their cigarette ends in the dustbins near the back door. Even the functional part of the grounds were well kept, which reminded Flo "Eh! we get to meet Fred the gardener tomorrow. I have to say he does a cracking job dunt he?"

"I can't disagree with you luv, the gardens are lovely"

They walked over to the laundry room and Fred's adjoining shed, as they rounded the corner toward the washing lines, they came across a wooden table with four chairs.

"This must be where the housekeeper and her hubby sit out" said Alice, and Flo sighed

"What's up?"

"I was just thinking that if I'd taken them up on their offer, it'd be me sitting out here of a summer's afternoon"

"Ah, but it would have been spinster childless you, cos no way would Bob have come here"

"For the second time this year, you're not wrong Alice"

"Oy cheeky!"

Flo smiled at her best friend. She might be an idiot on occasions, but, she couldn't imagine life without her, she checked her watch, "Are we going in then? I want to warm that telly up before I start on the sandwiches. There's a good programme on tonight"

"Do you mind if I just sit here for another five minutes?"

"Of course not, I'll see you inside" and with that Flo headed towards the house. Alice remained in her seat, listening to the blissful silence, you had to go to the cemetery round her way, if you wanted a bit of peace and quiet. She hadn't heard a single bus trundling past here, the convenience of living close to a bus stop was often canceled out during rush hour or when two turned up at once. She thought of Mrs Basker and her husband, and smiled at the irony of a *two bus turn up*, leading to her and Flo being here, she stood up and looked towards the house, the tops of the trees in the front garden visible beyond the roof, their leaves made a whispering sound in the summer breeze, the gentlest of whooshes to provide the perfect soundtrack to an August Sunday, she gazed up at the building itself, noting the frosted glass of the bathrooms and wondering how see-through they were at night, her eyes quickly moved to her and Flo's bathroom on the ground floor *'Remind me never to pee without the curtains closed'* she said to herself, and directed her attention to the upper half of the building again, she could see where the family room window, now the storage room had been bricked up *'It spoils the look of the house a bit'* she thought, her natural urge to find something negative, coming out even in such serene surroundings, she sniffed in disdain at the new bricks and not even the scent of the flowers nor the lazy buzzing of bees could make her feel any shame. Then, something caught the corner of her eye, she looked slightly left of the storage room and found herself looking at the window of room three, there was movement again and Alice squinted, she had good eyesight, only recently needing glasses for reading, but whatever it was, it had glistened, in the now low, sun's reflection, flashes of something silvery danced on the window, and then, one of the small clouds that dotted the sky, none of them close enough to touch, drifted in front of the sun, and Alice could see more clearly.

The glistening had been caused by a Tiara...On a head...A long Platinum blonde haired head...Rasputin had a woman in his room! Alice dived off the chair, and walked speedily towards the house *'I bloody knew it'* she murmured to herself as she strode through the back door. *Tell me I'm imagining things now'* she quickened her pace as she shouted,

"Flo? Flo? Flo? where are ya? Flooooooo?

CHAPTER 13

Flo came flying out of the the housekeeper's room into the corridor "Bloody hell what's all the noise about? you've just woken half the dead in Southern cemetery, get inside" she hissed,

"He's got a woman in his room!" Alice hissed back "I bloody told ya, but you didn't believe me!"

"Shurrup and calm down you daft cow!"

"Don't you swear at me!"

"Try and make me!" And with that, Flo rolled her eyes "Good God! I'm getting as daft as you. All this arguing is getting us nowhere, we sound like a pair of wailing banshees, now let me put the kettle on whilst you calm down, an' then tell me properly" with a deep sigh Flo headed back to the rooms, pulling Alice along with her. Sighing herself, and with her voice now at normal volume, Alice said "I don't need to calm down, and I don't need a brew. I need you to come with me to room three, now!, 'cos *he's* got a *woman* in there"

"Alice, we're going nowhere til you've told me, *calmly,* why you think he's got a woman in his room"

"She'll be gone by the time anyone listens to me" replied Alice, in a churlish manner. Fighting to maintain her own patience with her friend, Flo attempted to placate her

"*Look*, if he *has* got a woman in there, she's not going anywhere without us knowing. We'll hear the front door ding-dong if they go through it, and the back door's locked. Other than her climbing out the window and even then, we'd see her from our window, I can't see how she could escape unnoticed, do you agree?" Begrudgingly, Alice did and sat somewhat reluctantly at the table while Flo poured them both a cup of tea. With cigarette lit and biscuits to hand, she was ready to listen to Alice's *Fairytale* "So go on then, tell me all about this woman?"

Alice recounted her story of the glittering tiara, whilst Flo sipped, smoked, nibbled and listened.

"So are we going to his room or not? It specifically says *no* visitors of the opposite sex, and *no* couples. We're christian people Flo, we can't live under the same roof as an adulterer!"

'You managed it for the few months you were wed to Eddie' Flo muttered to herself "Hang on a minute, I'm thinking of a reason to knock on. He is a paying guest at the end of the day, we can't just go marching in his room accusing him of all sorts, without proof"

"My eyes are proof!"

"Remember when you thought you thought you saw Maggie Price's husband canoodling with a woman in your back entry, and it turned out he'd bought a job lot of mop heads with sticks and was carrying them home?"

"It was foggy!"

"He had a lump on his head for weeks, cos she listened to you and just went for him as he walked through the door"

"Is it my fault she's got a temper? And it's not foggy today, I know what I saw, there was definitely a woman in his room"

Flo sighed "so you're sure about this"

"As sure as can be!"

"Well, give me a minute to think of something *Flo scratched her head-* "could it've been Miss Henderson? She might have knocked on to borrow summat?"

"She's more of a yellowy blonde -you can tell that's out of a bottle an' all, the woman I saw was even tartier"

"Alice! Sally Henderson looks anything but a tart!"

"Her hair says different -No the one in *his* room was platinum, like that Marilyn Monroe, she won't last, they don't make 'em like Mary Pickford anymore, now she was classy"

"Never mind film stars -an' you call me for liking telly! Right, I've just thought of something. I'll knock on" said Flo getting up from the table.

"I'm coming with you" insisted Alice, standing up as well. Flo sighed again, "Okay, *we'll* knock on and *I'll* say the guttering's leaking or summat like that and there's a damp patch downstairs directly under his floor , Where *is* directly under his floor? Asked Flo thoughtfully. "Hang on I'll check" Alice got up and left the room to return a few moments later "his room window is over the painted door in our corridor, "Perfect" responded Flo, "the guests don't come through there, so he won't know we are bare-faced liars, wanting a nosy in his room"

"You'll be thanking me when we get rid of that cad! He could be the George Haigh of the North, for all we know. Only the ugly version"

"Do you think Haigh was handsome"

"For a murderer? yeah!"

"You're not normal, well, come on then I want to watch telly. Let's get this over and done with...And let *me* do all the talking"

"I won't say a word"

Flo hoped she meant it but experience told her otherwise. They began what she considered, a fruitless journey, to room three. As they traveled up the corridor she felt obliged to say, "For God's sake Alice, stop linking me, we're not thirteen!"

"I'm scared!"

"Go back then, I can handle it"

Alice removed her arm from Flo's and tutted "I'm not that scared, and it was *me* that caught him out"

"The only thing you've probably caught is the wrong end of the stick now shut up and let me talk"

"We'll see" muttered Alice under her breath as Flo rapped on the door smartly.

"Who is it?" came the gruff reply

"It's Flo, Mr Poole, the stand in manageress, erm we've got a leak downstairs directly under your room I need to come in and check your" *she searched for the right word* "pipes" She shot Alice a 'what *have* you got me doing?' glance

"Can it not wait til tomorrow?" said the still gruff voice

"We could be like Noah in his ark by then" piped up Alice. Flo gave her a dig "It'll only take a couple of minutes," she replied, with a warning look to Alice

"Give me a minute, I'm not decent"

'He can say that again!' mumbled Alice. as they heard drawers closing and general shuffling about, "he's probably hiding her as we speak" Flo said nothing, just continued giving her friend the 'death stare'. After a few minutes Mr Poole came to the door wearing a dressing gown over his day clothes "I am trying to rest" he said

curtly "I know, and I'm extremely sorry sir" replied Flo "we just need to check this leak, may we come in?"

Mr Poole said nothing in reply, but, he opened the door fully and stepped back to let them in Flo and Alice looked around for the 'leak'

Except for the three of them, the room appeared to be empty. "why are you looking in the wardrobe?" he exclaimed, as Alice pulled open its doors. Flo replied "erm the leak might be dripping on top of the wardrobe so she's just checking if inside is damp. Can you feel anything wet Alice?"

"Nope, dry as a bone. We need to check the floorboards remember"

"Yeah, you can do that, you're nearer the ground than me"

"The *floorboards*?" Said Mr Poole with a confused air

"That's right" replied Flo, just to check that there's no bod - I mean dampness" She watched as Alice dropped to her knees. "You'll have to shift them suitcases Alice"

"I'll do that" he said hurriedly and bent down to pull the two suitcases out from under the bed.

Alice crawled around feeling for dampness as far as the guest was concerned but in reality, for the lumps and bumps of displaced floorboards. It was as smooth as a baby's bottom. A somewhat disappointed Alice stood back up

"Nowt there" she said with a confused look that only Flo noticed

"Well, we're sorry to have disturbed you" she said backing out the door with a firm grip on Alice "we'll be back up in a short while with the tea-time sandwiches"

"Just knock and leave them outside the door," was the terse response as the door closed in their face. Alice began to speak but Flo hushed her and led her back down the stairs. Not a word was said until they reached the kitchen and Flo had shut the door behind them.

"I'm having you 'seen to' when we go back home, you're imaging things. A woman in his room? where was she Sherlock?" demanded Flo.

Alice shrugged. She knew she'd seen someone, never bloody mind that she wasn't there now, she *had been* "well, Florence, in the time it took *you* to get up there he could have melted her in acid already"

"And *where* was the vat? On his soddin window sill ? Just stop judging people and jumping to daft conclusions"

"I know what I saw!"

"Just shurrup and start sorting out these butties. There's a good play on at tennish that I want to watch"

"What's it about"

"Don't know I've never seen it"

"How do you know it's good then?"

Flo looked at Alice in disbelief "*You've* got no room to talk , when it comes to things you haven't seen!" she argued.

Alice by now starting to doubt if she did see a woman , but equally insistent to herself, that she did, said nothing and started plating up. She'd have a proper word with Flo later when she was more relaxed and better inclined to listen.

With the tea time trays delivered Flo said "I'm going to have my bath before supper time. Do you want yours first or second?"

"I had one on Friday before I came here!"

"You've got an indoor though, I couldn't be mithered getting the tin bath out so, I had a strip wash"

"Well, I tell you what, so I don't get out of me routine, you have yours first, then leave the water in for me and I'll jump in and out"

With bath time sorted, the ladies sat down to their own cake and sandwiches and both enjoyed them thoroughly. Maureen was a grand baker and a fine cook, they both agreed on that.

After their baths and with pinnys over their dressing

gowns, both women escorted each other to deliver cocoa and collect the tea trays. Mr Pooles tray was outside his room with a piece of paper on which he'd requested *no cocoa, and no disturbances please*

"He could have said before we made it" grumbled Alice

"Why, is it weighing you down?" mocked Flo, although secretly she agreed with her friend, '*how soddin rude*'

It was a different story at Sally's door, she too was wrapped in her dressing gown and had obviously had a bath, she insisted that no-one collect her cup she would wash it out in her sink and bring it down in the morning.

With the guests settled for the evening and no one expected, Flo saw no harm in locking up for the night, and at just after eight thirty she and Alice settled down for what she hoped would be a quiet night in front of the telly.

The first hour was blissful. Flo caught the last half of something with Jimmy Clitheroe in it and laughed herself silly, whilst Alice caught up the the goings on of Don Carlos in her book '*The Spanish Cad*' Just before the play was about to start Flo said, I'll stick the kettle on, Alice nodded and carried on with her book.

A few minutes after that, just as the tea was brewing the noise began. "someone's flushed the bloody toilet" exclaimed Alice in between the clattering and rumbling of the pipes"

151

"Well, it is only a minute or two after the curfew"

"*After* being the operative word Flo, and it can only be one of the two of 'em, my money's on *him* or whatever tart he's hiding"

Flo resisted an overwhelming urge to shake some sense into her,"Alice we've discussed this til we're blue in the face"

"Okay, you don't believe me about the woman but I bet it's him flushing the toilet to try and get back at us for disturbing whatever vile things he was getting up to" she cocked an ear in the direction of the corridor, "the pipes are still rumbling, I'm gonna go and check the toilet on his floor, cos the cistern will still be hissing" and without waiting for Flo to reply, she dashed up the corridor.

It was a determined Alice that threw open the door to the first floor bathroom to be confronted by absolute silence and no sign whatsoever of it having been used. She stood with furrowed brow for a few seconds, a tad dismayed she'd read Sally wrong. '*Mind you* 'she thought to herself '*anyone who bleaches their hair, has to have a sluttish side.'* She made a mental note to have a word tomorrow, because it didn't make sense to climb another two floors. If it wasn't him, it *had* to be her, and eager to find out if Don Carlos had won the duel with Enrique for the hand of Emily she started back down the stairs. As she reached the second step, she thought heard a woman's sobs and stood rigid on the steps, not even daring to breathe, all her concentration centred on listening. In the quietness she heard it again, muffled but definitely a woman crying, and it seemed to be coming from Mr Poole's room. She took the remaining steps two at a time, and charged up the corridor

"What's up?" Asked Flo as her friend stood before her gasping for breath, "did you run to the top of the house?" Alice waved her hand in a wait a minute motion and gradually her breath came back.

"Flo, as God is my witness, and you know I don't blaspheme, I heard a woman crying in *his* room" seeing her friend's lips start to pucker and her eyes narrow, Alice continued, "before you start, answer me one question *Who* do I love more than anyone else in the world?"

"Yourself?"

"Be serious Flo. I'll give you a clue, it's a film star, *not* someone I'm related to"

"I'm glad you added that last bit 'cos I was convinced your Uncle Bert was big in Westerns!"

"Flo! You're wasting time! *who* is my favourite film star"

"I don't know you're so choppy changy sometimes...erm...Rudolph Valentino?"

"Got it in one! Well, I swear on his life "

"Can I just point out he's been dead for years"

"That's not the point! Okay then, I *swear* on his grave"

"You swear on his grave?" Flo stared directly at her friend. Alice was a woman who took her love for Rudolph seriously

"I'll put me hand on a bible if you want? I definitely heard a woman crying in that murderer's room"

You heard a woman crying? And you swear on Rudolph Valentino?" Flo knew when her friend was deadly serious. She might be mental, and imagining it, but, she was deadly serious " Right c'mon, we'll knock on"

The two women marched forcefully up to Mr Poole's room, and Flo rapped on the door. It was a determined knock. After a few moments the door opened and a disheveled and sleepy looking guest stood before them, he'd opened the door wide enough for them to see he was the only occupant, his rumpled bed showing he'd been sleeping in it . Flo's face took on a mortified look.

"I am *so* sorry Mr Poole I meant to knock on Miss Hendersons door, I've got a ... a knitting pattern she wanted. I just got confused , being new here and erm" she was being to feel a tad foolish. Mr Poole stared at her for a moment, but, his only response was to close the door in her face, with a bang!

The walk back to their rooms was conducted in complete silence Alice's thought filled with '*I could have sworn*' Flo's with '*If she says one word I'm gonna murder her*'

Without a word, Flo switched off the TV, waited til the dot had disappeared, *they could blow up if you didn't do that.* picked up her cigarettes and an ashtray, gave Alice the dirtiest look she could muster and walked silently to her room, where the door was slammed. Alice knowing better than to attempt to talk to her, and still dealing with her own confusion about the events headed to her own room, where three more chapters of *'The Spanish Cad'* helped her fall into a fitful sleep

***

Throughout the house stillness reigned, disturbed briefly by the gentle sound of a woman weeping.

CHAPTER 14

The alarm clock went off at four thirty on the dot. She could have stayed in bed for another hour but Flo was excited and a little nervous. Today was her first day in complete charge. There was a new staff member to meet, Fred the gardener, and the two remaining residents she'd yet to meet, Messrs Hawkins and Parkinson, and later that day the new guest was expected. She'd also risen earlier than need be, in the hope of getting a few minutes on her own to have her brew and first cigarette of the day in peace, but as she filled the kettle she heard Alice's door open

"Are you up?"

"If I'm not you'd better start screaming 'cos you're seeing things"

Alice tutted at Flo's sarcasm and looked at the clock, "Bloody 'ell did you wet the bed? I thought we didn't have to get up til half five?"

"You don't" was the surly reply. She was still fuming with Alice about the shenanigans of the night before. She didn't want Doctor and Mrs Howarth coming back to an empty guest house, because Alice had offended them all into leaving.

Alice was seemingly oblivious to her mood, but in reality

experience had taught her that the best way to get Flo out of a mood was to pretend there wasn't one, "Well, bags I the bathroom first, are you brewing?" She disappeared into her bedroom and came out with her toiletries bag and flannel and headed to the bathroom. The evening they'd arrived Flo had unpacked and left her bathroom needs in the *actual* bathroom,which was what any sensible person would do. Not Alice, and she was still struggling to explain to Flo's satisfaction what it was that prevented her from doing so

"Have you got anything valuable in there"

"Well, the soap is from kendals and *Evening in Paris* talc doesn't come cheap and I've also got me you know whats"

"What you know whats" Flo asked, knowing full well,

"You know!" Alice's voice had got higher and her expression had reddened "Me you know what, you know whats"

"Box for your dentures?" She was enjoying Alice's embarrassment

"*No!* They're on the sink over there"

"Get *them* out of here" Flo shouted in horror

"You'll realise when your time comes" her friend replied, "and it's only the bottom set"

"I'll be keeping mine when the time comes, *touch wood*" she tapped the tabletop "on the bedside table in a glass, like normal people"

"Wait til you trip up going to the sink to tip the water out. *you'll* be leaving 'em there. Anyway, I meant further south, me doings"

Flo having briefly forgotten what they were talking about in the first place looked mystified until it 'clicked' what Alice was referring to

"Your sanitary towels?"

"Bloody ell Flo, walls have ears!" Alice went a bright shade of red, having always been prudish about such matters. Unless it concerned anyone else, then, she didn't mind spreading the word about menstruation..

"You should have seen the state of Ann from the Chippy. She must have got her visitor whilst on the bus. I was walking behind her. I was a bit further down when the bus pulled up. The funniest thing was, every one on the bus was gawping out of the window at her. She always sits at the back, what a view they all got as she passed 'em. She must have thought they all fancied her"

"What do you mean the funniest bit? That's a bloody awful thing to happen., 'scuse the pun. I hope you told her"

"I tried, but she gave me a dirty look before I could

speak , so, I left it to the lads in the pub she went in"

By the time Alice had had a cat-lick and returned, a pot of tea and toasted crumpets sat at the table, enough to satisfy them til breakfast proper Flo was also dressed. In answer to Alice's raised eyebrow, her reply was "If you can leave your teeth on the sink, I can have a wash in it"

A glance at the clock told her it was time to get a move on, by now, her mood with Alice forgotten, she said "come on get dressed, we've got work to do. I'm going to brush me teeth, meet me outside the bathroom. A few minutes later both women headed for the kitchen, as Flo switched the light on, because it was still a little dull outside she said to Alice "Ok then Madame de toilette, go and flush for England"

"I thought we were taking turns?"

"Okay then, you make a start on breakfast for nine" She didn't even care that Alice saw the smirk on her face

I'll flush" she replied sulkily, eyes narrowing, she'd lost this round but not the battle, she had no intention of flushing toilets everyday, and if she ever found anything more than a number one, well, it didn't bear thinking about. Which is exactly what she did, and having a weak stomach, she found herself *heaving* as she went up the stairs. By the time she reached the top floor she was expecting to be met by an over flowing toilet bowl, the bathroom however, was spotless.

Although all the rooms were uninhabited for the night she did the same with the bathroom on the second floor, and used the opportunity to pop into Philip's room to see if he'd left it tidy. She was slightly disappointed to find he had. When Flo was boasting about all the things she'd taught him as a child, she'd have loved to have been able to respond

"You didn't teach him tidiness very well"

On the first floor she tip toed warily to the bathroom, and swung the door open quickly as if expecting to find someone there. It was empty and tidy. She gave the toilet chain an extra hard yank as if that would make it any louder than it already was, and was just about to leave when something caught her eye and made her scream. A creature such as she'd never seen before, she ran out of the bathroom and straight into Mr Poole, which made her scream again. Without a word he barged past her into the bathroom and locked the door. She hesitated for a moment and then knocked before saying

"Erm Mr Poole. There's a big creepy crawly on the floor" She shuddered at the thought of the slug like hairy thing she'd spotted near the sink

His voice came through the door. "I'll get rid of it. No need to worry"

He was almost 'nice' *'Suit yourself'* she thought and after unlocking the dining room and outer doors, went back to the kitchen where Flo had breakfast well underway. The smell of bacon was delicious. Flo instructed her to check the toast and hummed Glenn Miller as she attended to the hob.

A blind eye was turned to the amount of breakfast cooked when the minimum of guests were having it, as was usual each Monday morning, it'd had already been paid for whether they partook or not and happy staff were good staff. '*If I ever have staff they'll be as happy as Larry'* thought Flo, as she tossed the twelfth sausage in the pan.

Soon the trays were loaded and with Alice following behind with the tea trolley they headed to the dining room, where both Sally and Mr Poole were at their respective tables, her with a book, him with one of the newspapers.

Flo told them both to remain seated and took their orders, as Alice poured tea, then leaving them alone to enjoy breakfast, they both popped into the office to check the to-do book and get their breath back, it'd been a hectic but enjoyable start to the day, and now was the perfect time for Alice to tell Flo about the creature in the first bathroom

"Flo, there was a massive creepy crawly in the bathroom on the first floor"

"Thank God for that" said Flo in mock relief, "for a

moment I thought you were gonna say there was a woman chopped up in the bath"

"Ha, bloody ha... No, really, a massive one, I was just about to come and get you"

"Get me? What could I have done?"

"Well, you're always saying you're in charge-Anyway, *he* came out of his room, practically pushed me over in his haste to get to the bathroom"

He must have been bursting to go"

"Stop making excuses for him! You'd blame yourself if Jack the Ripper murdered you and have a whip round to buy him sharper knives"

Flo tutted at her daftness and flipped through the to-do book "The only thing that's odd" she said looking at the written instructions "is Monday not being the big wash day"

"I thought that myself" responded Alice, when in fact she'd paid no mind to it at all. She took her laundry to the wash house. It passed the time better to have some gossip whilst one mangled one's sheets, and fancy machine or not, there was no-one to gossip to in the laundry room

"Ah! it's cos of Fred the gardener, Monday's his regular day and I suppose sheets flapping on the line would get in his way -Oh! I know why now, he burns the rubbish on a Monday. I thought I spotted some scorched bins behind his shed"

"Well, keep the windows closed, it'll cause havoc with my chest. I wish you'd mentioned that before we came. I didn't think to pack any camphor"

"Stop moaning, he's not gonna burn it in your bedroom, have you seen how far away the shed is?"

"Listen, I know it's bigger than me backyard, but it's hardly Old Trafford football ground is it?"

"Don't let Bob hear you say that!"

"If he did I'd be getting in touch with 'The News Of The World'...*Man hears woman talking, from miles away*"

"You know what I mean! You can't even say the word 'United' in our house. Between you and me, our Joyce prefers them to City, she told me"

"What did you say to that?, cos your Bob's a blue, through and through" to herself, Alice thought '*I bet he was fuming*'

"I told her to keep her gob shut if she still wanted a Dad in her life" and at this, both ladies cracked up laughing and spent a few minutes joking about the dirty looks they got from Bob when City lost. Neither was mithered about football the way he was.

The ringing of the reception desk bell alerted them to Miss Henderson and Mr Poole both ready to hand their keys in and head off to work. A cheery goodbye from Flo and silence from Alice, and both left for their working day. Another cough from the staff entrance alerted them to a rugged looking man, handsome in an ugly way, a bit like Humphrey Bogart. Tall, and lean with the bronzed complexion of someone who worked outdoors.

"You must be Fred" said Flo" with a smile to match his "I'm Flo and this is Alice"

"How do ladies" he replied with a touch to his cap. "I won't come any further, I've got my outdoor shoes on, but if you need me to do anything later, just let me know"

Alice contemplated asking him if he could pick a padlock, but kept her mouth shut. Flo replied "Well, you just carry on luv, I'm sure you know what you're doing, and can I just say, the grounds are beautiful, you do a cracking job," and with that, Fred gave another touch to his cap, smiled proudly and headed off to attend to his work. As soon as she thought he was out of earshot, Alice started taking the mickey

"*You do a cracking job*" she said mimicking Flo. "You don't half creep"

"It is *not* creeping, it's called being nice. You should try it sometime. Mind you, he's not bad looking is he? and he's our age. Play your cards right and you could be heading for your second marriage"

Alice looked as indignant as she could manage. Folding

her arms, she said, "I beg your pardon? Why on earth would I be interested in a manual worker?"

"Cos you've still got a bit of life left in you. Don't you want to get wed again?"

"If I did, it'd have to be someone with standards!"

"Like your philandering last husband?" said Flo a tad cruelly. Alice's back stiffened, and she venomously responded. "he might have been a philanderer but he was a philanderer with an office job and a good pension. I *wouldn't* need to work away for a month to buy a twin-tub, I could buy one now if I wanted" Her tone was as savage as Flo's was cruel, she almost always gave, as good as she got.

The ringing of the phone saved her from anymore of Flo's wrath. It was Philip checking they were okay. Flo assured them they were. *Yes,* she'd remembered the new guest. *No*, there wasn't anything she didn't think she could manage. As they were speaking Lily and Liz popped their heads through the staff door to wave hello, and then went about their duties, and Flo had a cunning idea to get Alice out of her way for a while "Alice, one of us needs to do a stock count and one of us needs to supervise the girls whilst they do the rooms so, choose whichever you want"

The last part was a blatant lie, but Flo knew Alice would choose that option.

"I'll go with the girls then," she had an ulterior motive apart from not having to count spuds. She could have a proper root about in room three.

"Well, just hang on here and mind reception whilst I nip to the loo" Flo said, hurriedly coming out from behind the desk and doing the *'dying for a wee'* dance. She didn't need the toilet at all, she needed to warn Liz, who was in the dining room. Making sure the door closed behind her, she turned left instead of right and hissed at Liz

"Come here a minute" she said in a conspiratorial tone. Liz, looking curious, came over. "Listen" said Flo, "I've told Alice to come and *'supervise'* you two. I know you don't need it, but she's getting on me nerves and I have to do a stock count before nipping out to get bread and milk for tomorrow"

Liz laughed and said "No worries Flo, we'll cope with her"

A relieved Flo replied "I just needed you to know, that she isn't really in charge, cos she'll be the first to tell you"

"Like I said, we'll manage. And why don't you ask Fred to pop out for the groceries? He won't mind at all"

"Oh, that would be a blessing. I'll ask him. I'm meeting meself coming back at the moment and I want everything to be alright"

"Don't fret" said Liz and laid a comforting hand on her

shoulder "You're doing a grand job" Flo gave a deep sigh of relief and smiled, a smile that said '*Thank you. I needed that*'

"Right, I'd better go, she thinks I've gone for a wee. I'll tell her to meet you upstairs" with that a more relaxed Flo headed back to reception to find Alice writing something down.

"The phone rang whilst you were on the toilet. It was Doctor Carter the new guest. Talks like someone related to royalty, lovely accent. Anyway, he'll be arriving at about six. He asked what was on the menu for dinner so I told him it was Chedder et Onion avec pastry"

"It's cheese and onion pie!" said Flo in a frustrated tone

"Oh Flo, don't you read anything but Titbits? That's *French* for cheese and onion pie, you daft apeth. Doctor Carter knew what I meant, but that's the high classes for you, he seemed very pleased too"

"It's only a bloody pie! Right, off you go to supervise. I'll see you down here later"

"Ta-ta for now" said Alice, still in snob mode. Flo thought she seemed a bit too pleased to get off, but didn't have time to worry about she was up to. Liz and Lily would keep their eyes on her. She got out the stock record book, with diagram and instructions from Philip attached and headed to the stores to make a start.

Alice made her way to the top floor and found Liz in the bathroom.

"Immaculate as ever" said Liz with a smile, referring to Sally "If all the guests were this tidy, we'd have no job"

"Gives you time to concentrate on the areas that need it" replied Alice "I've noticed some of the skirtings could do with a dust. Anyway, don't mind me, I'm sure you know what your doing. I'll leave you too it, and come and check on you in a bit. I'm just going to check, the, erm, light fittings on the first floor. They've been making funny, erm, noises"

Liz realised why Flo had prewarned her. If she hadn't one of them would be getting thrown over the banister and it wouldn't be her "You're the boss" she said straight faced, and Alice smiled in confirmation. She turned to go, but a thought occurred to her, and she turned back

"Liz?"

"Yes?"

"Have you ever noticed any funny goings on, on the first floor?"

Liz looked puzzled "You mean with the light fittings?"

"Erm, yes. But in general too"

"Can't say I have" responded Liz, still perplexed

"Ever have any, erm, funny guests?"

"Tommy Trinder stayed here once, but it was before my time"

"No, I didn't mean funny *ha, ha*. I meant funny *peculiar*"

Liz furrowed her brow, as if thinking. "You'd have to ask Mr and Mrs Basker about that. They've probably seen everything, being in this trade for years. We don't really get to see the guests except in passing at weekends, so I couldn't say"

"Oh," said Alice "okay, keep up the good work and don't forget to check them skirtings, I'll see you later" with that she headed to the first floor. '*Well, that explains why no else has noticed he's a strange one*' she said to herself. '*but he can't fool me*' she added smugly as she let herself into his room.

Right 'Rasputin Haigh' let's see what you're trying to hide!

CHAPTER 15

Monday afternoon saw the return of Misses Tippet and Barker, they arrived just after lunch and Miss Tippit did all the talking.

"Which one are you then, Flora ? Or fauna?" She smirked at her own cleverness. Miss Barker, a far nicer woman than her friend, winced. Alice, who's favourite job had already become to sit behind reception reading Tatler, looked up from pretending she was writing up some important paperwork, and said

"Funnily enough, me mam and dad were considering calling me Flora, after Flora Macdonald, cos me dad, and *this* was before he died, said he needed a lifeboat when her waters broke" She lowered her voice to more conspiratorial tone " *We're all girls here*" she raised it to normal level again "but can you imagine if they had?" she looked at Miss Barker as if awaiting an answer "Erm, no" came the shy yet warm reply from a smiling mouth, Miss Barker was enjoying this. Miss Tippit most definitely was not. *Her* lips had almost disappeared, under the weight of the pursing.

"Well me best friend, the other manageress" and to herself she thought *'cos let's have it right luv. I'm not the maid. I'm management!'* "she's called Flo, been called that since I've known her, and there's no way I could go round with someone called Flo, if *I* was called Flora, that's *asking* for bother. I'd have shunned her from the start" she paused, both for dramatic effect, and to think of what to say next, "And then I wouldn't be here, would I?" She smiled her most insincere smile towards Miss Tippet.

She'd worked her out from day one, she was a bully and a snob, but beneath it was an air of commonness. And even though there was a certain irony in Alice's contempt of Miss Tippet, there was no part of her that was a bully. *Her* friendship with Flo was a balanced one, they took turns to get one over on each other, that's what real friendship was about. Miss Tippet was the kind to talk over the quiet- *and what was the word?* serene! Miss Barker, both Alice and Flo had agreed on that. She made you feel 'interesting' too, with her twinkling blue eyes and the shy attention she gave you.

"Anyway" continued Alice, do *you two* have first names?"

"Yes we do!" snapped Miss Tippet. now, may we have our room keys?" she glared at Miss Barker as she heard her quietly add "*please*"

Without a word Alice turned to the key cabinet, and plucked out the keys for rooms one and two, she held them out in the palm of her hand and Miss Tippet picked them up as if trying to avoid any form of contact with Alice's skin. Glaring at her, she said

"Neither Miss Barker nor I will require dinner but cocoa will be expected at the usual time" and with that she stormed off, Miss Barker leaned forward and whispered *"We've got a hamper of goodies to finish off. I'm Lucy and she's Abigail"* and with that she turned and headed after her friend. She was a decade or more, older than Alice and Flo, but, she walked with the ease of a much younger girl and the glide, Alice had seen, at the pictures, of young ladies attending finishing school. Alice would have loved to go to finishing school, sometimes she practiced walking, in her parlour, *you needed a posh room to do posh things in* with two or three books on her head, but the most she had managed was four paces before the books fell off. Having said that, she could only walk another half pace before a piece of furniture or a wall brought her to a stop.

She still had the smirk on her face about Miss. Tippet's discomfort when Flo returned to reception.

"What's put a smile on your face? have you offended somebody?" Alice put a hand to her chest in mock surprise. "Moi? That's French for *me,* by the way

Flo rolled her eyes and said "I thought you didn't like the French?"

"I don't it was only them stood between us and Hitler, and they let him in. I blame them for the battle of Britain. The French language is too good for them if I'm honest"

"So who've you offended?"

"Not a living soul...Flora?" she laughed at the in-joke.

After the total disappointment of the morning, when she'd had the opportunity to conduct a thorough search Mr Poole's room, and had found absolutely nothing of an incriminating nature save evidence of his dire taste in clothes, *his suits would have been sniffed at in the demob section,* she'd been a little down in the dumps. The thought had crossed her mind that she might well have been seeing things and as for the crying woman's voice? Sally was a strange girl and who's to say it wasn't her, sound traveled in big places, she remembered getting lost once when her and Flo were at London road station, and somehow she managed to find herself on the wrong platform and Flo was over at the far end, but she could have been in next doors back yard as she'd heard Alice the first time she shouted "*Flo! I'm over here"* Maybe she was judging him on his utter ugliness? She'd never admit it to anyone, not to even to herself, but Alice tended to judge a book by its cover, and many many times she got the contents completely wrong.

Yes, the run in with Miss Abigail Tippet had certainly put a smile on her face and it was a contented Alice that sat down for her mid afternoon break with Flo, and after a tasty lunch of bubble and squeak they'd settled down with a brew and a cigarette whilst Mario Lanza serenaded them from the radio.

"Fred's a lovely man" said Flo

"Thinking of marrying him yourself are you?" Flo hit her friend playfully on the arm with her cigarette packet, "don't talk daft. The man isn't born who could woo me away from my Bob" she paused "If you don't include Gary Cooper" she added with a wink. "no, I meant as a person, and you should be thankful too, he's gonna do the daily run for bread and veg. He only lives a mile away, so even on his days off he's gonna pop round and use the van to get what we need in. It'll save us having to lug it back on Shank's Pony" and then, changing the subject completely she asked Alice "Eh! Why did you call me Flora before?"

Alice filled her in on the incident with Miss Tippet, and Flo nodded her approval "I can't stand bullies. Lowest of the low. You did well luv" Alice basked in her friend's approval and feeling magnanimous in her triumph added "I might have been wrong about Rasputin"

"Well, I never" gasped Flo in mock surprise "Alice Clough admitting she might have misjudged someone! I never thought I'd see the day"

"Shurrup you daft sod" replied Alice cheerfully, she was really enjoying herself, not that she'd admit it, but apart from the odd night she'd slept over whilst Flo was expecting Joyce, and one or two overnight stays in Blackpool and Rhyl, this was the longest the best friends had spent together since meeting. The work was easy, the staff were acceptable and she loved the evenings. Her reading, Flo watching telly, but both able to multi-task by chatting to each other at the same time.

The tinkle of the front door opening told them someone was here, and both made their way to reception to find themselves looking at the debonair David Parkinson who was charm itself in Alice's eyes

Six foot tall, slim build, with dark hair, and with a slim mustache complimenting a handsome, upper class English looking face, he was immaculately dressed in an obviously expensive suit, nowt like the *rags* in Harold Poole's wardrobe. Alice melted.

"Good afternoon ladies" he said, taking both their hands at once and giving each a delicate kiss "I have returned from the beauty of the countryside, to be met by an even more beautiful sight, and I may now be forced to stay here every weekend, for what can compare with the vision I see before me" Alice giggled, Flo smiled her professional smile and said "Welcome back Mr Parkinson, would you like your room key?"

"I most certainly would" he replied

"Get Mr Parkinson's key" she said to Alice, who was just stood gawping.a nudge in the ribs told her Flo was speaking"

"Sorry, what did you say?"

"Mr Parkinson's key!"

"Oh! yes, here you are sir, Can I get you anything else?"

"No good lady. That will be all" He headed for the stairs and then turned as if suddenly remembering something "Just to let you know, I won't be home for dinner. Other plans" and with that he winked and headed up to his room.

"He is lovely" said Alice, once certain he was out of earshot, "I'm not over keen meself" responded Flo. Alice looked a little confused at the role reversal "What's up with ya? It's usually me not taking to people"

"It happens now and again" she shrugged "I didn't like your Eddie from the start, remember?"

"You never said!"

"I bloody did, *you* never listened and I feel like that about him" She glanced at the clock "I'd better let Maureen know there's one less for dinner, you mind the shop I won't be long"

"Happy to" replied a cheerful Alice, picking up her magazine, secretly hoping for another glimpse of Mr. Parkinson, whilst she was on reception, '*such a pity he was a married man*'. She thought.

Flo returned within fifteen minutes and said it'd had come as no surprise to Maureen that he wouldn't be in for dinner, he rarely was. She was about to share

Maureen's theory that he was a *gad about* with the ladies, when the front door opening alerted them to the presence of who could only be Chad Hawkins, who couldn't have looked more American if he walked in singing *Yankee Doodle Dandy,* with the stars and stripes on his head.

A little shorter than David Parkinson, but bigger built and wearing a loud check suit and a Stetson, the floor seemed to shake with every heavy footed step he took towards them, with a touch of his brim, he introduced himself

"Howdy ladies, I'm Chad Hawkins" he said,without offering his hand. In fairness he was holding luggage and bags in either hand. Flo returned his greeting and offered assistance with taking his bags to his room which he was happy to accept"

"That would be mightily helpful maam" he replied.

Neither woman could fault him on manners. "Assist Mr Hawkins with his bags please Mrs Clough?" she said to an initially eye narrowing Alice *'Why should it be me?'* being her initial thought, but the next thought *'I might bump into Mr Parkinson on the way down'* had her agreeing with pleasure. "I'd be delighted to, Mrs Holden" and she grabbed the key and one bag and led the way for Mr Hawkins

"Oh Mr Hawkins" Flo said as they were walking away "Will you be in for dinner?"

"Unfortunately yes" was the reply. Chad Hawkins found English food a little unappetising, he longed for home, and a proper juicy steak Texas style

'Cheeky sod' she thought as he walked off. *Some people don't know what good food is.*

Alice returned a good few minutes later. "did you hear him?" asked Flo still fuming "*Unfortunately yes!,* and not a word to Maureen" she warned "'cos if someone said that about my cooking, they'd be wearing it"

"I won't" agreed her friend. He gets on *my* nerves a bit,. he was waffling on about all sorts, started showing me his souvenirs from Hadrians wall, all of it was tat. He'd apparently nipped over the border and bought a couple of kilts but he could only find one when he opened the bag, started blaming some negro who worked on the train he was on, Said it must have been him that thieved it"

"Some what?"

"Negro or was it nigger? She searched her mind, "anyway, whatever it is that they call coloured people over there"

"Well, we bloody don't and I'll thank you not to say words like that in my presence. Do you remember Charles that coloured soldier? The one who came round to mine a couple of times after he helped me when me bag burst and me shopping spilled on the bus"

"I never met him did I? But, you never shut up about him,

so I felt like I had"

"Oh no you didn't did ya" said Flo, recalling the incident "He got off even though it wasn't his stop and helped me all the way home. Our Joyce was with me, she was only a nipper, she was fascinated with him and he gave her a bar of chocolate, she thought it was Christmas in July. Well, me point is, he was a lovely man, studying to be a doctor when he went back home. American films have us thinking they're all maids and servants but they're not"

"Ooh, can they be doctors?" asked Alice ingenuously. Flo bit her tongue and merely said "Just don't use that horrible word again, and if I hear him use it, I won't be responsible for me actions, there's no way the doctor or Mrs Howarth would stand for it either, anyway, come on we've got work to do and the new guest is due in a few hours"

The rest of the afternoon passed in a hive of activity, Sally and Mr Poole arrived home at their usual times, both heading straight to their rooms, nothing was seen of the other residents so Flo and Alice had a tidy up of the reception area and having realised she'd forgotten to give the guests their post, Flo asked Alice to knock on with their letters. Sadly there was nothing for Mr Parkinson so no excuse to knock on his door, but she merrily trotted about giving the other residents their post. Flo had asked her to apologise for the lateness of the delivery, but she didn't. They should consider themselves lucky to be getting a door to door delivery.

Outside rooms one and two she looked carefully at a hand written envelope with a red wax seal on the back. She read the name , which was in posh calligraphic hand writing, '*was that Barker or Basker?* She couldn't see Miss Barker getting such an envelope. She *was* judging again but surely this time she was right, and it wouldn't hurt to double check that it wasn't indeed for Mrs basker Flo wouldn't be best pleased, if she gave a guest correspondence meant for the manageress, she placed it back in her pinny pocket and headed back downstairs to find Flo had got them a pot of tea and some biscuits.

Now that all the guests were in residence, they took their breaks in the back office rather than their rooms, to be on hand should any assistance be needed.With their little break finished, Flo remained in the back office, she was expecting a call off Philip and had paperwork to do, whilst Alice remained front of house, eagerly awaiting either a glimpse of David or the arrival of Doctor Carter

At five past six, the new guest made his entrance and a few minutes later a shell shocked Alice entered the back office

"I think you'd better come out here a minute Flo"

"I'm in the middle of all this" she said pointing out the pile of paperwork in front of her "what is it? You look like you've seen a ghost"

"Not quite, can you come out here"

Flo tutted and stood up "it'd better not be any daftness"
She said as she got up from the desk and went to find out
what Alice was 'going on about'

There before her stood a handsome young man, in his
late twenties but younger looking. He was tall with
beautiful brown eyes, the shiniest dark hair and dressed as
impeccably as Mr Parkinson if not more so. He was also
very obviously of Indian descent. Flo gave him a big smile
as Alice muttered "This is Dr Carter, only it's spelled K, h,
a, t, t and a"

"Hello doctor we've been expecting you. Did you have a
good journey"

"I did actually" replied the doctor in his cut glass and very
English accent "The weather was fine, and the train ride
unhindered by stoppages and such, he put his hand inside
his jacket and pulled out an envelope from his breast
pocket "Before I forget may I leave this with you for
Doctor Haworth, I do expect to meet up with him upon
his return but it is a letter from my father and I wouldn't
like to misplace it"

"Certainly" replied Flo taking the envelope from him. I'll
put it in the safe for safe keeping" she smiled at her little
joke then continued "I understand your father and the
doctor were in the army together?" The sharp intake of
breath from Alice said '*You knew ! and you didn't tell
me!*' She'd deal with her later

"Not quite" the young doctor replied "Doctor Howarth was stationed in India with the British Army and my father was a newly qualified doctor. They were introduced at a party and found they had friends in common back in England. To cut a long story short, it ended up with my Father being offered his first job as assistant and translator to Dr Howarth, and became the start of a lifelong friendship, even more so when my father and mother came to live in and open a General Practice in Hertfordshire, which is where I was born"

Flo knew the story but was enjoying the look on Alice's face "Well, I'm sure you'll want to freshen up before Dinner. If you just sign in there, I'll get the key and show you to your room. Is that all the luggage you have?" she said referring the one suitcase he had beside him"

"My trunk is following on and should arrive tomorrow" he replied, picking up the case and following Flo. Alice had remained silent, but as the pair disappeared she gulped, now she'd got over the shock of him not being as 'English' as she thought, she'd have to tell Flo the rest of what Mr Hawkins had said cos he wasn't going to be best pleased at his new neighbour

'It's gonna kick off is this' she thought to herself as she waited for and *dreaded* Flo's return.

CHAPTER 16

Flo came trotting down the stairs with a grin on her face "Before you say a word Alice, yes I knew he was Indian, I just wanted to see the look on your face. And it's your *own* fault, when Philip offered to tell you how to spell his name you got all offended"

"I thought he was insinuating I couldn't spell, anyway never mind that, I've got something to tell you"

"If you've seen Mr Poole walk past with a body, I don't want to know" Alice rolled her eyes and sighed "I wish it was that! right now I wouldn't mind asking him to murder me 'cos I think we've got trouble and Fred's already gone so we're Man-less"

"I'm not sure that's a proper word" responded Flo with a grin "but I'm not sure you're right in the head either, what's the bloody matter with you? and who's gonna cause trouble?"

"We'd better go in the back," replied Alice with her serious face on, Flo sarcastically made an '*After you*' motion of her arm and followed her into the office

Sitting at the table and lighting a cigarette, she said "Go on then, what've you done?"

"It's not so much what I've done, it's more what I've not

told you"

"And *what* haven't you told me?" replied Flo pausing between each word, her eyes getting narrower with each syllable

"Half of what Mr Hawkins said"

"Come again?"

"In fairness you did tell me to shut up when I was trying to tell you more" Alice said defensively

"Tell me more *what?*" Flo was getting frustrated

"Well, he had a bit of a wobbler when he noticed the kilt was missing, started going on about how we're too soft with n- that word you said I shouldn't say, in this country, and how back home the 'that word again' knew their place and wouldn't dare to rob a white man or they'd end up hanging from a tree"

"And what did you say to all that?"

"I didn't know what to say I just stood there a bit gobsmacked, what was I supposed to say?"

"Something like '*We don't stand for that kind of talk round here'* You've more or less let him think you agree with him, he'll be inviting you to his next lynching! are you not reading about what's going on over there Alice? It's awful, they're not even allowed to drink out of the same tap as white people or sit next to them on the bus"

"Well, I do believe we should stick to our own"

Flo looked furious "Say that again?"

"Look at Marjory from Arran street, the one who married the Italian lad, she can't even hold a conversation anymore without flapping her arms about, and she doesn't do it right cos she wasn't born doing it, she knocked over an entire display of cornflakes in the Co-op the other day... and eight kids? She's not even Catholic"

"You get on my nerves sometimes" said Flo with a disgusted look at her friend "Well, Mr Hawkins is in for a surprise if he thinks I'm like *you*. This is Manchester England, not Al -a -bloody- bama, we do things differently here, if he's not happy about any of the other guests he can find somewhere else to stay, and I mean it"

As *'luck'* would have it the phone rang, and it was a friend of Chad Hawkins asking her to remind him a car was picking him up to join said friend for dinner.

Flo sent Alice to give him the message and just sniffed when she returned with his 'apologies' for forgetting and ordering dinner. When he came downstairs some minutes later she walked into the back office and left Alice, or Eva Braun as she was now going to refer to her, to deal with him. The showdown between bigotry and humanity was delayed for a day or so.

At dinner time, Flo introduced the doctor to the his fellow residents dining that night, polite how do you do's were said, Miss Tippet asked if he knew people in Bombay who were once neighbours of hers. Dr Khatta coming from some thousands of miles further north, politely said he's never lived in that area. Mr Poole asked what field he worked in and everyone was impressed to hear he was going to be a surgeon, and then as is common in English society, with which the British born doctor was very familiar, everybody went back to their meals and totally ignored each other except for small talk between courses.

It would turn out to be another week before Mr Hawkins and Dr Khatta's paths crossed. In that first week, both were busy working, all hours. Hawkins because the deadline for installation of the machinery was looming and the doctor, because he was new and learning the ropes at his new workplace.

That first week of Flo and Alice's tenure, flew by and by the time weekend came around they felt like old hands. When Friday arrived, Hawkins informed them he was leaving straight after work to visit the lake district and see where Shakespeare lived. Flo didn't even bother correcting him, stupid got what stupid deserved. Dr Khatta rang to say he'd be having dinner with friends and staying over til Sunday evening, which was a bit of a relief because it turned out that he didn't eat meat, well not their meat, meat like kosher meat, which you *could* get but it meant a trek to Cheetham Hill, the poor lad had lived on veg and potatoes all week, it wouldn't be so bad the week after, because Maureen had sorted out a menu with extra fish dishes and a veg hot-pot thing when they had the proper one. Alice couldn't understand how he was still alive "I've never heard of people not eating meat before"

"He does eat meat, just meat that's like kosher meat"

"Bit strict int he? I know loads of Jews who enjoy a meat pie"

"They're not proper religious though are they. He obviously is"

"I wonder if he goes to church?"

 Flo groaned "Come on, let's lock up and go and watch some telly, I'd wanted to use the washer, but we'll do our own washing tomorrow"

She'd easily picked up how to use the washing machine in the laundry room and had been delighted at the swathes of sheets drying in the summer wind, she'd do a big wash for her and Alice tomorrow, as it looked like it was going to be a quiet weekend. Bob had sent a postcard to assure her all was well with him and Joyce, and neither had withered away without her, only four guest would be remaining for the weekend, and she'd told Philip he needn't come over, a fact for which he was very grateful as the work on Father's new bedroom wasn't going as smoothly as expected. All in all, Flo anticipated her second weekend in charge would be a more relaxed affair than the first.

The next morning the ladies awoke dressed and commenced their duties with a barely a word said between them, they hadn't fallen out they were just confident in what they were doing and keen to get on with it. The four remaining guests Misses Tippet and Barker, and Sally and Mr Poole were all waiting in the dining room when breakfast was served, after the guests had been seen to, Flo and Alice joined the others in the kitchen for their *brunch* as Alice informed them , was the correct name for what they were eating, pointing to an article on appropriate brunch wear in one of her posh magazines, the pinnys they were all all wearing didn't feature in the article.

After helping to clear away, Flo and Alice with laundry bags in hand, headed towards the laundry room. As she emptied out her laundry bag Alice noticed the letter she'd failed to deliver to Miss Basker and hurriedly put it onto the pocket of the pinny she was wearing. As the large machine chugged away she asked Flo "So, how long does it take?"

"About an hour"

"In that case I'm gonna nip to the loo"

"Take your time, I'm going to sit outside and get a bit of sun"

Alice having decided the letter was addressed to Basker

not Barker and she was going to open it, 'cos they'ed been told to open any post addressed to her unless marked personal - *well, Flo had been told that, but she was sure they'd meant her as well* -needed somewhere she wouldn't be disturbed to read it, and where better than the bathroom. To her chagrin she found the bathroom locked and a voice came through the door "Is that you Aunty Maureen ?I've got me little visitor so I'm just having a proper wash"

Alice shuddered with disgust and headed to the office, where Lily gave her the fright of her life as she popped out from under the table where she'd been sweeping up crumbs. She thought back to earlier in the week when her and Flo were having a chat with Fred over a brew, after spotting him coming out from behind the painted over door, where he'd given them both the fright of their lives as neither had thought of it as being a real door that led somewhere

"So what were you doing behind that door. We didn't even know it worked anymore"

Fred had laughed "*Well it doesn't go anywhere anymore but it has its uses"* he told them, how when the house was in its original condition, it was the back stairwell used by the servants to access the family room on the first floor which he reminded them was now a bathroom, a storage room and guest room three. Harold's potential as a mass murdered had been forgotten by Alice, in the wake of the Hawkins versus Khatta goings on, and in her eagerness to read the letter, he was forgotten once more, behind that door would be the perfect place to have some privacy, she recalled Fred saying he was the only one who went in there now, as it was used as a storage area for certain supplies, and the key was kept on the wall at the side of the key cabinet, she found it and slipped it into the keyhole, the door opened easily, she found the light switch to the left, switched it on, and closed and locked the door behind her. A quick glance around showed a flight of stairs to the left, obviously leading nowhere and stacks of boxes to the other side of it , taking a seat on the bottom step, she pulled out the letter and opened it

Dear Lucinda It began

'Lucinda?' she thought, what a daft name, and she carried on reading

I've known where you are for a while now, but I also know that whilst father was still alive there was no hope of a reconciliation, but as you may know ... ...

Alice read on, slowly becoming aware of what was being said and about who

Oh my God, we're practically in the presence of royalty, she thought, wait til I tell Flo, she'll go mad at first, but wait til I tell her. An excited Alice headed for the door, she listened carefully to hear if anyone was in the corridor and when she thought the coast was clear she reached for the light switch and switched it off. The corridor remained lit, but *where* was that light coming from?

A glow from the top of the staircase intrigued her, and she stepped back from the door, leaving the light off and headed to the top of the stairs where, forgetting what Philip had previously said, she was somewhat surprised to come across another door with no door handle and the light was coming from under the bottom. It didn't take a genius to work out that it was room three and this was confirmed when she got on her hands and knees to peep under the door and saw the padlocked suitcases underneath his bed, she was just about to get up when she saw something else, a woman's legs and feet in a pair of stilettos, *I was right all the time wasn't I? Well this time I've got you mate!* She slowly backed away from the door, tiptoed down the steps holding her breath, and out of the door. As soon as it was locked she bombed it back to the laundry room, it was empty, Flo was sat outside,even better!

"Flo"

Flo jumped slightly startled "Bloody 'ell I was miles away, int it lovely out here?"

"Yeah it's great, Listen to me, and promise not to get mad"

"Why what've you done" she replied with pursed lips and folded arms.

"Nowt, just do something for me. Look up at the house

and keep your eye on the window of room three. It's that one there" she pointed to Mr Poole's window"

"I'm not daft! now *what* am I supposed to be looking at"

"Keep watching you'll see"

Both ladies sat and stared at the window, and within moments someone came into view. It wasn't Mr Poole"

"Was that?"

"Yes Flo a *woman*. He mustn't be fussy, this one's a brunette and she's got big ankles, I saw them"

"How?"

"Come with me"

In slight shock and feeling somewhat embarrassed that she hadn't believed her friend, Flo followed meekly behind, she could only manage to raise an eyebrow when Alice opened the door, that wasn't a door, and quietly obliged when Alice made a shushing motion, nothing would surprise her now, and *that* Mr Poole would be getting a good talking to, if not asked to leave, rules were rules. Over-acting a tad, Alice led her on tiptoe up the stairs and pointed first to the door and next to the gap at the bottom miming the actions to *'take a look under there'* Flo got down on her knees and looked

"I can't see anything the room looks empty"

"Let me see" said Alice dropping to her knees and pushing Flo out of the way, she got up almost instantly "come on he's probably seeing her out as we speak.

Paying no mind to how much noise they made the two women rushed in the direction of reception, it was empty, a quick look outside revealed nobody, Just then Liz came through and the ladies did their best to look casual

Liz smiled and headed to the staff quarters only stopping to say "Oh Mr Poole's just popped out, to the shops I think he said, I've hung his key up"

"That's nice of you" said Flo still slightly out of breath "erm was anyone with him?"

"No, he's the solitary sort int he? You can tell" and with that she went through the door.

The women stood in silence for a few minutes Flo spoke first "Don't be gloating but I owe you an apology, can't doubt what I saw with my own eyes. Now we've got to decide what to do about it"

"I think we should call the police"

"And say what? He's got rid of her now?"

"But *how* has he got rid of her"

"Oh come on Alice, I accept he's been somehow sneaking women in his room but he's not Bluebeard. They're probably just tarts"

"Well, I'm telling ya Flo, he's murdering 'em. Look at him, he oozes 'oddness' and he's ringer for Haigh"

"Looking like a murderer doesn't make you one"

"Women disappearing from your room does though. And don't forget the rules say *no* visitors in rooms"

"Well, for that reason , and that reason only, Miss Marple! we'll have a good root around next time he goes out to work. We can't risk it now, he could be back any minute, we'll see if we can open one of the padlocks, that might tell us more about him. You may be right, he does seem to have something to hide"

"*He's not the only one*" mumbled Alice to herself remembering the letter, but that could wait til another time "We *could* have a root round whilst he's in there with one of 'em" she said to Flo.

"Aren't you scared of him murdering you?"

"Ha, bloody ha! I don't mean us being in the actual room, but I've had an idea. To herself she said, *and we'll need Fred's drill*"

She filled Flo in with her idea, leaving out the bit about the drill and Flo partially racked with guilt agreed to everything she said, they'd have to bide their time and wait for the opportune moment but they still had a couple more weeks.

As they finished discussing their plan. Misses Tippet and Barker came downstairs and headed for the residents lounge. Flo could have swore she saw Alice do a curtsey but it had been a long day. That night Both ladies found it easy to fall asleep. Flo cos she was absolutely shattered, Alice cos finally someone believed her about *him*.

By Sunday evening all the guests but Mr Hawkins had returned from their weekend out. He always returned from his weekend sightseeing trips on the Monday evening and they still had to deal with his reaction to Doctor Khatta, if any, Alice *had* been known to exaggerate, although something told Flo, that in this instance she wasn't. After serving the evening cocoa, both her and Alice decided to have an early night.

At around four o clock the next morning both women were woken by the sound of someone flushing the toilet. both came out of their rooms at the same time.

"I'm gonna put the kettle on" said Flo in a resigned tone "We're up now, it doesn't make sense to go to back to bed"

"I'm gonna have a look what floor it's on" said Alice, in an angry tone "cos someone's getting read the riot act, we can't have this every morning" She marched off before Flo could say anything. Flo left her to it, she needed a brew and a cigarette before she could think straight.

Alice marched purposely up the stairs. All silent in the first floor bathroom, ditto for the second. It had to be either Miss Henderson or Doctor khatta. She wasn't wrong, the cistern was still hissing. she'd have words with them both individually, after breakfast. As she turned to go back downstairs she thought she heard singing coming from one of the rooms. She stood still and listened, the sound was coming from the doctor's room. She crept closer to the door to try and make out what the tune was. It was unlike any song she'd heard before, like some form of chanting...Like witchcraft...or Voodoo. *Bloody 'ell* she thought *can we not have a normal guest? Wait til I tell Flo this one*

"Well who was it?" Flo asked on her return, she was sat at the table with a cup of tea warming her hands and her soul. She wasn't really interested but it was inevitable she was gonna be told something, by the look on Alice's face

"I'm sorry to have to tell you this Flo, but your dear young doctor is not normal too"

"What makes you say that? cos to be fair, he is new, he might have forgot about the no flushing rule"

"Never mind the flushing, Hes doing voodoo up there"

"Come again?"

"Mumbo jumbo, black magic, call it what you will, *I've seen* Tarzan, he's doing God knows what, up there, you want to hear the noises coming out of his room, I couldn't make head nor tail of it and you know me and listening through doors. I'm usually spot on or nearly there, this was all a foreign language"

Flo said nothing, just shook her head. It was going to be one heck of a day. She could feel it in her water.

CHAPTER 17

On Monday morning for the first time since they'd
arrived, apart from the odd bit of 'spitting' the
Wednesday before, it rained, and it rained buckets. Flo
imagined the flowers opening their petals wide for a good
drink, even with Fred's love and attention, some of them
had begun to wilt a little, scorched by the sun that had
shone for two weeks straight, apart from the
aforementioned 'spitting' She loved the rain, more so
when she was in than out, but, there had been days when
a walk in the rain had saved her sanity, after a daft row
with Bob, or an even dafter one with Alice.

Fred unable to work in the grounds, busied himself
around the house, wearing his indoor shoes and a long
brown overall on top of his clothes. It was half day
closing for the shops so he'd done the shopping early, he
intended to spend the rest of the day, catching up with
the interior of the house's needs. With step ladder in
hand, he replaced light bulbs, fixed the leaky tap in Miss
Barkers room and generally contributed to keeping the
guest house in tip-top fashion.

As the guests left for their day of work, there were
invariably cries of "*Oh my goodness look at the rain*" or
"*Oh my it's pouring down out there*" as they each opened
the front door to leave, the only person not to say
anything was Mr Poole, who just pulled his coat collar up,

pulled his hat down and legged it without a word of goodbye, to his car

"You'd think he'd be gentlemanly enough to offer the ladies a lift to work"

"Him? Gentlemanly?" scoffed Alice "That's a foreign word to the likes of him. I'd say that not getting a lift, was a life saver. Look at all them people who went to Sweeney Todd for a shave, they didn't expect to end up in pies did they?"

"What has *that* got to do with *this* situation" asked an incredulous Flo

"Both murderers" she replied as if stunned to be asked such a stupid question and then in her own inimitable way changed the subject completely and without warning as she had on many occasions, and in many places including her neighbour's deathbed

Aw, Gladys I came as soon as I heard. How is he? I'm not gonna lie he looks terrible. Should he be breathing like that?"

To be honest Alice, I'm glad of the noise, we were convinced he'd 'gone' at least six times yesterday. His breathing was a quiet as a mouses I was worn out with it. But the doctor's told us it's not long now, we're just hoping he hangs on til his Bobby gets here. They couldn't stand each other, but if you can't make up your differences on your deathbed when can you?"

You're not wrong Gladys. So, how are your Corns?"

"Eh, Flo, what would you do if Royalty was staying here?"

"What *are* you waffling on about now?"

"Just imagine we had a royal guest?"

"Which one?"

Alice seemed hesitant "Erm, no one in particular" there was shiftiness in her reply, but Flo didn't notice.

"Bloomin eck *you* asked the question! The queen? One of her kids? A cousin?"

A relieved Alice said "Oh I get you, erm, say it was Princess Margaret?"

"Well, as long as she observed the rules and paid her bill I wouldn't have a problem" She noticed the smirk on Alice's face and added "Why are you asking? Do you know something I don't? Has she phoned to book a room, or is it you jumping to conclusions again 'cos someone with a posh voice called Margaret phoned?"

"When do I make assumptions?" asked an indignant Alice

"All I'm saying is *Doctor CARTER!*! now come on we've got work to do, can you go and sort out the newspapers and magazines in the lounge, give the old ones to Fred, he burns 'em, I'm going to give the office a going over, as Alice was about to leave, the phone rang.

Flo picked it up and her 'face' made Alice know, there was something going on. Her replies to whoever she was talking to were terse, and her face looked fuming

"Yes...Really?…are you expecting her to Call?…and *that's* what you want me to say?…Bye" She slammed the phone down and looked livid

"Who was that?" asked Alice, partly in concern for her friend who was obviously upset, but mostly out of nosiness

"Mr Debonair, also known as *him!,* David bloody Parkinson" she almost spat out his name

"Well, what's he said to get you so mad?"

"How many times was he in for dinner last week?" Flo grabbed the guest request book and flicked through the pages "*Once!*" she exclaimed "The man's an adulterer" She spat out the last word and her expression was one of disgust"

"You've worked all that out 'cos he went out to dinner? and you *call* me!"

Flo gave her friend a withering look "I've worked it out 'cos the cheeky beggar's just asked me to lie to his wife"

Alice's eyes grew wide with curiosity "why, what's he said?" She moved closer to Flo knowing this was a hushed voice kind of conversation. Flo seemed to have forgotten in her temper, because her booming voice made

Alice jump and wiggle her finger in her ear

"Have you spoken to his wife yet?"

"I can't say I have" replied Alice, still rubbing her ear and thinking *if I get earache it's your fault*

"Well, I *have.* She phones of a Monday to check he got back safely, and once or twice she called in the week to ask me to pass a message on. Lovely girl. anyway she heard me say something the other day, and asked me if I was from Sheffield, can you believe that?" without waiting for Alice to reply, she continued "I've lived in Manchester for more years than I lived in Sheffield and she could tell. Turns out her Nanny was a Sheffield lass. I've proper took to her" She paused, her face getting red with anger, her voice louder. Alice stepped back a pace or two "And *that*" She searched for the right word, but couldn't find it "male... *JEZABEL* want's me to tell her he's working to a deadline, cos he's *NOT* coming back here tonight!, I'm *LIVID*!"

"You wouldn't know it" muttered Alice before patting Flo's arm in an attempt to calm her down "Well, what are you gonna do if she phones?" She took a deep breath before her next sentence "He *is* a guest" she winced waiting for a blasting from her friend, but Flo, having had a eureka moment, calmed herself down, smiled and said "There's more than one way to skin a cat, Alice. Now get the lounge tidied up"

At four o clock Mr. Hawkins returned, arms full of packages, this time neither woman offered to help him with his bags, if the atmosphere was frosty he didn't notice it, he was coming to the end of his time here and was looking forward to going home, for decent weather and decent food, the two things England lacked in his opinion.

The rest of the day went to routine, Philip called to confirm he'd definitely be over at weekend, and would try to get some photographs developed so Flo and Alice could see how the building work was coming on.

In the blink of an eye or so it seemed, it was time for dinner to be served and for all hell to be let loose...

It being the second Monday of Cook's set menu, dinner that evening was toad in the hole, using up Sunday's leftover Yorkshire pudding batter, poor Doctor Khatta having to settle for just 'hole' with extra mash and cheese sauce instead of gravy, Flo fretted that he'd wither away without any meat and made a note to ask Fred to nip to Cheetham Hill one day and get him a couple of chops. The soup was tomato and pudding was jam roly poly with custard, both women looked forward to sitting down to theirs once the guests had been fed and watered.

The last person in the dining room was Chad Hawkins. Too hungry to bypass the unappetising fare that was always placed before him, although in fairness he had a fondness for the sweet and stodgy puddings, jam roly poly being a firm favourite of his, if only the main courses weren't so bland. His mouth watered at the thought of a juicy steak,. not long to wait now, he'd soon be back in the good ole U S of A

He took his place at his designated table, and looked around to give a fellow guests a nod of hello, he'd been here long enough to know that 'at the table' conversation was frowned on. The English liked to eat their dinner in peace, saving their words for polite conversations in the lounge. As he looked around at his fellow guests whilst waiting for his soup, his eyes fell on Dr khatta who smiled and nodded. Both his smile and nod were not returned, as a furious looking Chad Hawkins stood up and made his way to reception.

Both Flo and Alice stood behind the desk. It was Flo that addressed him. "Can I help you with anything Mr Hawkins?" she asked, knowing full well what his *problem* was. His voice oozed hate as he replied

"Ma'am where I come from, a white man is not expected to sit in the same dining room as a nigger"

"But you're not where you come from though are you? You're from where I come from, where *we* come from" She calmly replied, looking at her friend "and to be honest it doesn't bother us who sits with who, does it Alice?"

"Not really"

Flo shot her friend a dirty look and she quickly added "I meant *NO*, not at all"

"So, now we've cleared that up" continued Flo, gaze firmly fixed on Hawkins "Is there anything else I can help you with?"

"Yes" he replied, returning her gaze and with a menacing tone in his voice "Get that nigger out of here"

Alice tensed up and grabbed Flo's arm but Flo was forewarned and forearmed, she smiled 'apologetically' and leaned forward on to the counter

"I'm sorry, but, *that* isn't going to happen sir, but I'll tell you what *is*" She paused and placed her hand on his "*You* are going to pack and *leave* this establishment - Oh! by the way have I mentioned my Parents are Jewish?" Chad Hawkins immediately recoiled from her touch. She laughed and dinged the bell on the desk, and the forearmed part of her plan, Fred, came out of the back office looking stern and very able to look after himself if it came to fisticuffs "did you want me Flo?" he asked "yes, Fred luv. Could you escort this '*gentleman'* to his room whilst he packs and then please escort him off the premises"

"It'd be my pleasure" he replied coming out from behind the desk and standing too close for comfort to Hawkins who like many of his ilk, was only *'hard'* in numbers and two mere women or not, he was very outnumbered here

Alice, as surprised as Hawkins at what was happening but dead proud of her friend could only stand there with her mouth wide open as Flo continued "Let me tell you something Mr Hawkins. I'm well aware of people like you, we call them Nazis, now you Americans might be daft enough to spend years fighting them, then decide to become them but we do things different here. This is Manchester luv not Mississippi. We only hate idiots. Now I'll thank you to get your vile self out of this guest house. *You* are *not* welcome here!"

"I wouldn't stay here if I was paid to, and my company will be in touch for a full refund" he replied angrily

"Yeah, tell your boss to get in touch and I'll sort that out. I'm sure he values one racist salesman's opinion over the valuable ongoing contract, said salesman has been boasting about. *every bloody time* he's been in the lounge. Now *SOD OFF!* if you'll pardon my French, or don't you like them as well?"

Both Flo and Hawkins knew it was over. And Flo had won. He turned and headed up the stairs to his room, with Fred close behind.

Alice was still open mouthed. Liz having had the sense to close the dining room doors when she heard a commotion, popped her head out of the corridor and winked at Flo and mouthed and mimed *"I don't think they heard anything, but I did"* she laughed, gave Flo a *thumbs up* and returned to her duties.

Alice had finally got her voice back "Wow Flo, what was all that about?"

Flo sighed and gave a weary smile "I knew what was coming luv, so I had a word with Fred and he agreed with me that I was doing the right thing, if Doctor Haworth or the Basker's had been here they'd have sent him packing too"

"Do you think he'll really want his money back?"

"He won't say a word. He's been made to look a proper fool by a couple of woman and a gardener, and Doctor Haworth has got powerful friend in the NHS. Hitler Hawkin's boasting about the millions he's gonna make for his company, have bitten him on the bum. Right, you go and sort out our tea, and I'll join you as soon as they've finished in the dining room"

"You don't need to ask me twice, I'm shattered with it all, but, just let me wait til he's gone first"

Flo shook her head at Alice's nosiness, fortunately they didn't have to wait too long. Nothing at all was said by anyone as he tossed his key onto the counter, Flo called a taxi and Fred escorted him out to wait with him til the taxi arrived some five minutes later, realising it wasn't going to 'kick off' Alice headed for their rooms, to put the tea out, and when Fred came back in, he and Flo exchanged eye rolls, she thanked him for helping out and reminded him not to forget the dinner plated up for him to take home. It was coming to the end of a long day, only the cocoa's to do then she could relax for the evening. She'd planned to watch *The Good Old Days* but wasn't sure her eyes would stay open long enough. As she was just about to head to the staff quarters Doctorr, Khatta approached the desk

"And what can I do for you?" she said with a smile. He really was a handsome young man. If her Joyce ever brought a man like that to tea, she'd have no problem with it, although Bob might be a different matter, him being older and having dafter views, but they'd cross that bridge if they ever came to it. She thought of Hawkins' response to him, and shuddered, she couldn't understand how people could hate other people for no other reason than their colour or religion

"He, sighed and said "The incident before, it was about me wasn't it?"

"Noooo!" she tried lying, before sighing and saying "yes, but it's all sorted now, and he's gone. We do not tolerate that kind of behaviour here, and I'm sorry if you've been embarrassed in anyway"

"I'm far from embarrassed Mrs Holden. I'm extremely proud and honoured to know you, and if I can ever return your kindness you only have to ask"

"It isn't kindness it's common sense" she said matter of factly "we're all the same, and come to think of it, there is something you can do for me" There was going to be no good time to raise the issues of flushing the toilet, might as well be now "do me a favour luv and don't flush the toilet so early, it wakes the dead, and even worse, Alice"

He clasped his hands to his face "I am so sorry I completely forgot the no flushing rule, I awake early in order to perform ablution before I pray"

"Ab-what?"

"Ablution. I am a Muslim and am required to pray five times a day, before doing so I must wash my head hands and feet"

The penny was beginning to drop for Flo "do you pray out loud, in a funny language"

"Yes" he laughed "In Arabic"

"Well that explains a lot" She laughed as well "Alice thought you were - Oh never mind. Is it possible for you to do your ab -have a wash without flushing the toilet?"

"Consider it done"

"And one more thing" She winced "Alice is going to think you're like bleedin' Aladdin when I tell her, please don't get offended when she asks daft questions. Her heart's in the right place...I think"

"Doctor Khatta laughed a long and genuine laugh. I like it here, Florence, I like it a lot" and with that he bid her goodnight and headed to his room, whilst she headed to hers, exhausted, and wondering what else was to come. Running a guest house, certainly had its moments.

CHAPTER 18

Flo was pleased to see Beryl had made the fire, it added much needed warmth and cosiness to the room, it'd only stopped raining for brief moments that day and was positively 'tippling down again'. She was also glad that she'd insisted Fred take the van home and drop the girls off at bus stops with shelters.

The plates of food were still covered up on the table and Alice was just pouring a kettle of boiling water into the teapot "I was waiting for you to come" she said with a smile, an exhausted Flo plonked herself down at the table, too tired to need Alice's warning "*Mind the plates they're still hot, use a tea towel*" Alice sat down and removed her top plate, then passed the tea towel to Flo, for a few minutes they ate in total silence, Flo grateful for the peace and quiet because she really couldn't take another thing today, Alice pondering if now was the right time to bring up the letter.

After the meal was finished. Alice topped up the teapot whilst Flo scraped the plates and gave them a rough rinse, before stacking them on the trolley ready for a proper wash when she went to do the cocoa.

They sat down in their respective chairs and both lit cigarettes, Within minutes the calming effect of nicotine and the magical properties of a brew, had revived them enough to converse. Flo was the first to speak "It's been a bugger of a day hasn't it?"

"You're not wrong!" said Alice, I thought I was in a film when Fred came strolling out of the back office. Guess which film I thought I was in? It's not an old one and the actress in it looks a bit like me"

Flo rolled her eyes and smiled at the same time. Alice's strange normality was comforting. "I hate it when you do these daft riddles. I never get it"

"I'll give you a clue" she said nothing just turned her head slightly and stared into distance

"What *are* you doing?" Asked Flo

"Are you senile, I just told you what I was doing! I'm giving you a clue"

"Flo tutted "I give up"

"Aw, have a guess"

"The Hunchback of Notre Dame?"

"This is why I *hate* playing Charades with you at Christmas"

"I give up"

"It's High Noon"

"*High Noon?* what part of you, does Grace Kelly look

like?" asked an incredulous Flo,

Alice said nothing, she just stood up and turned so her face was in profile before speaking,

"Imagine someone's trying to strangle me, don't I *favour* her in that scene from *Dial M for Murder?* We only watched it the other day. I actually thought it was me on the screen"

Flo shook her head "*You* need serious help, are you sure no bombs dropped on your head during the war? And *how* was staring into space a clue for high noon"

"I was looking at the clock!" Alice's tone said that she couldn't believe no would have '*got it*' Flo let out a belly laugh, and didn't stop for a good five minutes, and even though Alice didn't have a clue what her friend was laughing about, she soon joined in as well, laughter was infectious they said, whoever '*they*' was, wasn't wrong.

"Thanks for that" chuckled Flo as she calmed down. "I needed a good laugh after the run in with Junior Adolf. Did you see the way he snatched his hand away when I said my parents were Jewish?"

Alice hesitated, she'd been known to say the wrong things in this situation "Stupid man...one look at your nose should have told him"

"Me nose?" questioned Flo, unconsciously touching hers

Alice panicked a bit. This was not going well "I only

meant the slight hook in it, should we do the cocoa? it's nearly that time" Flo's eyes narrowed a bit, but the call of duty overtook and she rose in agreement, it certainly was nearly that time.

As Alice washed their pots, Flo prepared the crockery and a tray of biscuits whilst she kept her eye on the large pan milk. With the scalding milk transformed into a pot of comforting cocoa, they headed to the residents lounge.

With Mr Parkinson out for the night and Mr Hawkins no longer in residence, the five remaining guests were seated in various places in the large but welcoming room, Miss Henderson was sat comfortably in a chair in readers corner, with a Jane Austen Book., Mr Poole and Doctor Khatta were discussing the fairly new National Health service and both appeared to be of the same good opinion of it, as their chat was interspersed with plenty of smiles. Misses Barker and Tippet were sat in their usual places, the two armchairs either side of the fire, which had been lit by Beryl and gave the room a great deal of warmth, they were both knitting and chatting, Abigail Tippets booming voice in comparison to her friends, drowning her and nearly everyone else out. She also had a way of slyly putting Lucy down whenever she ventured an opinion that didn't concur with her own.

Alice stared so hard at the women that Flo had to nudge her out of her fugue, and hissed at her *"stop staring like that, it's rude"*

Apart from Alice 'throwing daggers' there was a nice atmosphere in the lounge this evening, and if any of them, the young doctor excluded were aware of the unsavoury goings on of earlier on, no one showed a single sign of it. All the guests took up the offer of cocoa, with the three ladies electing to take theirs to their respective rooms, whilst the men stood up, bid them goodnight and returned to their discussion, Flo and Alice left them to it and headed upstairs for a while, during which Flo and Alice stripped the bed and checked for leftover swastikas in the Americans room. As they removed the sheets Flo quipped "I'm surprised he didn't cut holes in these sheets to feel more at home" It took Alice a few seconds to 'get it' but when she did she giggled, she was relieved to see the old Flo coming back, she wouldn't admit it, but, Alice knew the run in with Hawkins had hurt her. Footage of the concentration camps had had her in tears, and although Alice knew and probably secretly hoped 'cos everyone had their secret prejudices, that there was no 'Jewish' in *her* family tree, she'd been upset too, she wouldn't want to be one but, it didn't bother her if someone was and she couldn't imagine how anyone could inflict such horrors on another person.

With the newly 'available to rent' room ready for a proper going over, when the girls arrived the next day, they headed back to the lounge to collect the pots and damp down the fire. The gentlemen took this as their cue to retire to their rooms, and soon, Flo and Alice were ready to retire to theirs too. With a pan of cocoa to warm up on

the two ring burner, and all the other pots *soaking* for
Beryl. they made their way *'home'* and were soon in their
dressing gowns, relaxing in front of the still burning fire.

With neither mithered about telly, they put the radio on
for some background noise and pondered their own
private thoughts. Flo's being everything she'd have to tell
Bob when she got back home, Alice's being how to
broach the subject of the letter she'd convinced herself
she'd *'accidentally'* opened

"She's a nice woman" She said to Flo

"Who is?"

"Her, that Miss Barker, she comes across as a proper
lady"

"You're not wrong" replied Flo absentmindedly. Bob
would be fuming when she told him about the American.
He wasn't over keen on foreigners himself, but he was
even more not over keen on fools!. Nazis and Man U
supporters being in his top two. "I *know* I'm not" Alice's
smug voice, brought her out of her thoughts,

"Sorry luv, I was miles away. Say that again?"

"I *said,* I *know* I'm *not!*"

"Know you're not, what?"

Alice tutted "*wrong* about Miss Barker, being a *Lady*"

Flo decided to humour her, it'd been a long day "she is, she's got lovely manners, and a serene way about her"

"Almost like she'd been brought up royal, and attended finishing school" replied Alice with a smirk that didn't go unnoticed

"Who knows?" replied Flo "erm, do you know something I don't know?"

"Many things Florence, many things" retorted her friend with a big grin. Flo decided not to take the bait. It'd be some nonsense anyway, ignoring her friends last remark she imparted her view on Miss Barker's companion, "I'm not over keen on the other one, Miss Tippet., a bit loud mouthed to me, and have you noticed how she's always talking down to Miss Barker. She treats her like hired help"

"FLO! as God is my witness" Alice lied "I had the measure of her from day one. She's a snob! what they call *new money,* she's only loaded cos her dad did well with property after starting out with a market stall, she's just a generation away from working class"

"*You'd know*" mumbled Flo, but with affection.,Alice didn't hear and continued her tirade "in my opinion she's no better than she ought to be. You can hear the commonness oozing out when she talks. Miss Barker on the other hand, speaks like she's been raised royal" She smirked again, and again Flo decided to ignore it., she was too tired for Alice's nonsense.

"I'll see if we can dig out a spare crown from anywhere and pop it on her toast in the morning, now I don't know about you, but I'm going to bed. I'm shattered"

Alice decide now was not the time to produce the letter, a tired Flo was an extremely grumpy Flo and it had the potential to kick off...royally. She smiled at her in-joke and said "Should I damp down the fire then?"

"You do that luv. I'm gonna be out like a light as soon as my head hits the pillow,I'll see you in the morning"

"Oh!" interjected Alice "did you have a word about the toilet flushing? 'cos if I'm woke up at the crack of dawn again I won't be responsible for my actions"

Just as Alice had declined to mention the letter, Flo declined to mention her chat with the doctor. She just couldn't face the daft questions

"*Does he pray on a flying carpet? Has he got a turban, or a magic lamp?*"

"Yeah I had a word, it won't be happening again, goodnight luv"

"Good night"

The last sound heard that night, was the noise of their respective bedroom doors closing...

And in the main house, it was the sound of a woman gently sobbing...

The rest of the week passed in a flurry of activity, the sun had come back out, and all the signs were there for an Indian summer.

David Parkinson's wife had taken to calling most evening's hoping to catch him. Flo hated having to lie, well, she didn't actually lie, just said *"No he's not in yet"* he'd hardly been in at all and in between their chats about the joys of Sheffield folk, Flo could hear the voice of a woman, accepting of her *'fate'* and still very much in love with her husband, regardless of his foibles. It seemed he had at least one good point, that of being a wonderful and interested father, during his rare moments at home,on one of his flying visits back to the hotel to change and check his post, Flo practically hissed at him that it might be a good idea to ring his wife. He must have obliged because it was a cheerier Patricia *Mrs. Parkinson's first name and one she insisted Flo call her by* who phoned the Friday evening of that week.

She had begun to open up to Flo, during these calls, and Flo,having just seen the guest requests for the following fortnight had had the germ of an idea. One hour later after a common sense approach from Flo, which led to the *floodgates* opening and Patricia confiding in a 'stranger' on the other side of a phone line, a plan had been made, she'd have a chat with Philip when he arrived in the morning, it would mean moving him to another room, but she knew he'd agree. '*Yes Casanova*' She said to herself, referring to David '*I have found the perfect way to skin your cat*' she smiled and pondered whether to tell Alice now, or wait to see the look on her face when the new guests arrived, she decided on the latter.

Alice a tad miffed that her best friend seemed to be always on the phone, had amused herself dropping hints to a totally bemused Miss Barker, who could have swore she curtseyed every time she came near her, but she put it down to the knee complaint Alice was always complaining about. The *one* thing that *did* made her feel a tad uncomfortable, was Alice's obvious antagonism towards Abigail. Yes she could be bossy and she *was* a frightful snob, but Lucy had met worse, and she was genuinely fond of her miserable friend who patronised her, yet had genuine care, she'd even felt it necessary to approach Alice about her conduct on one occasion.

"She doesn't mean it, you know, when she shouts like that. She just doesn't like me saying silly things, and I can be very silly when I want to. Abigail keeps my feet on the floor, and I'm glad of that"

"If only she knew where your feet should be" Alice had replied cryptically and later on that day without a word of apology, she blatantly stood on Abigail's foot, as she was loudly chastising Lucy for not being too sure how the NHS actually worked, then flounced off with a '*bob*' to

Lucy and a filthy look to Abigail, thankfully unseen as she was dealing with the pain to her 'corn'

Although she'd have also liked an excuse to stamp on Mr Poole's foot, she kept her distance from him. Now he'd been exposed for the disgusting person he was, she felt itchy around him, and could barely contain her contempt for someone who had 'relations' with tarts! And even worse, sneaked them into respectable establishments. '*Mind you*' she'd thought, '*someone that ugly had no choice but to pay for it*'. She determined to catch him out the next time, and remembered her need for Fred's drill just as he was passing.

"Fred?" she called out in a coquettish way. "If I wanted to borrow your drill at any time, where would I find it?" She hoped she sounded casual

"Have you got something that needs attending to? because I've got a few minutes free now"

"NO! It's not that" she fished in the dark corners of her mind for a good excuse "I'm a widow as you may know" he did, it was her favourite topic of conversation at the kitchen table, *that* and her late husband's pension. "and it's sometimes hard to get someone to do the little jobs, so, I'm thinking of getting my own drill. I can more than afford it" Fred groaned inwardly, Flo was definitely the nicer of the two, how did she cope? "and, I was wondering if I could borrow yours to practice on a bit of wood or summat"

"Top draw of my tool chest in the shed. Help yourself"
he wandered off thinking '*What a strange woman!*'

Saturday saw the early arrival of Philip, impressed at how,
good the guest house looked, it appeared to be
immaculate inside and out '*Knowing Flo*' he mused '*the
bins have a had a bleaching out*'

A two hour meeting behind the closed office doors saw
both Flo and Philip come out laughing their heads off.

Alice more than a little miffed to be left out of their little
pow -wow "*It's nowt Alice*" Flo had assured her "*We're
just gonna be going over boring paper work*" had
comforted herself with the knowledge that she too had
her own little secret, and it was still burning a hole in her
pinny pocket.

.

CHAPTER 19

"You two have been as thick as thieves since he got here" Alice was referring to Philip, it was Saturday evening and having completed their duties early with Philip's assistance, the working day was now over and they were relaxing in front of the telly. The only guests in residence, were as usual, Mr Poole and Sally, no one was expected back til Monday afternoon and both women were glad of the rest.

"Well you're gonna find out sooner or later but breathe one word and you're dead"

"My lips are sealed" said an excited Alice, she *loved* gossip.

"You know I've been chatting to Mrs Parkinson a lot"

"I'm half expecting you to say she's moving into your house" Alice quipped. "Do you want to hear this or not?" said her friend in a miffed tone, before continuing

Their kids are eight and ten, and like me and Bob there's an age gap,he's ten years older than her"

"And the *rest* with you and Bob -sorry! go on?"

"Tut! I was stuck between the devil and the deep blue sea, you can't really divulge a guest's carryings on, even if he is a philanderer but, I didn't need to, she burst into tears one day and told me everything, so I had this idea"

She leaned forward and recounted her conversation with Patricia and the brilliant idea that had come out of it, during this, Alice, forewarned by Flo not to interrupt or she'd get told nowt, managed to keep quiet, too enthralled and somewhat impressed by how cunning Flo could be, her face however conveyed every reaction known to man from disgust, shock and horror, to amazement and delight, when Flo had finished Alice rubbed her hands in glee and said "I can't wait til Monday"

On Sunday evening Philip took his leave assuring Flo he had every confidence in her for the up coming week and the arrival of the new guests. After serving cocoa and before retiring to their own quarters they double checked the resident request book to check they had everything in hand for the comfort of their guests, both laughed at David Parkinson's request,

From Monday I will be on Annual leave and ask that I am not woken for breakfast. Tea and a slice of toast and marmalade at eleven o clock each morning that I am in residence will suffice.

"Yeah, like that's gonna happen" said Alice and both ladies cracked up laughing again.

Monday morning came and went without incident, Flo and Alice by now working like they'd worked there for years, whizzed through their regular duties. A staff meeting first thing, after the two guests in situ had departed for work brought all the staff up to date, Flo glossed over the identity of the new guests by pretending she didn't know anything other than it was a couple and instructed Liz and Lily to move Philip's stuff into the room formerly inhabited by Hawkins and prepare room six for the new arrivals. Fred, slightly surprised but willing to do it, had been asked to collect them from the station later that day. When Flo got him alone and explained why, he'd laughed a hearty laugh and had said "*You, Flo, are a rum buggar, and talk about devious! You should be running the country*" And they'd both cracked up at the thought of a Woman prime Minister "*It'll never happen, at least not in our lifetime*" Said Fred prophetically "*And if it does, she'll have to be more man than woman*" replied Flo, equally prophetically

David Parkinson had added a post script to his brunch request. On Monday afternoon, he would be returning from 'work' having been so tied up he'd been unable to return home the previous weekend. *The absolute cad!* And would it be possible to get some sandwiches and a drink upon his return, as he was heading out for a late dinner and overnight stay with 'colleagues'

At four o'clock he arrived home and Plan *'Con a Cad'* Alice's idea, was put into action

Flo kept conveniently out of sight when he arrived so as not to be faced with any "*Why didn't you tell me sooner?*" questions when all was revealed. At five thirty she asked Liz to collect his tea tray and ask if he could see her in the office as a matter of urgency.

Alice wasn't too pleased at having to remain on the reception desk but, Flo assured her the door would be left open enough for her to hear what was being said

As she took deep breaths and prepared for her *'performance'* she heard the creak of the door and looked up to see Mr Parkinson stood before her, the gulp she gave before speaking added to the authenticity of the performance, "Oh Mr Parkinson sir, I'd didn't even know you'd arrived home, or I'd have called for you immediately"

"What is it My dear?" he said with insincere concern, he'd assumed some hiccup in administration had led to his bill not being paid, it sometimes happened but he knew he had more than enough money, what he couldn't work out was *what* circumstances involving him could lead to the look of distress on the housekeepers face. He began to feel nervous, and that made him 'snappy

"Come on then woman! Out with it?'"

"I'm afraid it's about your wife, sir"

He felt his legs buckle slightly. Patricia was a good sort, and wonderful mother. Surely she wasn't? He felt the need to sit down

Flo continued "She called Friday, Saturday, Sunday, and first thing this morning, but we've been able to contact you"

A wave of relief washed over David, just before a wave of panic set in, thankfully she wasn't dead, but why all the phone calls? Patricia was usually such a sensible type, a good wife, an unquestioning wife. Had she found out about Phoebe? Or Clare? Or Holly? His attitude, clothed in guilt took on a more abrupt tone. "For heavens sake what is it? I have plans and need to get ready"

"It's your wife's mother sir, she's taken ill *She hadn't she'd just bought a villa in the south of France and Patricia was headed out there to stay with her for a week* your wife has had to leave immediately and was trying to contact you about the children. It's a highly contagious condition your mother in law has and the children can't be in contact with her, in case they get...Polio...So, they'll be coming here, she'd have told you if she could have gotten hold of you" *you philanderer!*

Parkinson looked dumbstruck "Coming here? what do you mean they're coming *here?* What about *our* housekeeper?"

"Apparently she's got the flu, sir...the really bad one, she's having delusions"

"Did Patricia not think to contact *my* mother?"

"I wasn't aware you had one Sir" *SON OF SATAN!* but,

now I come to think of it, I believe your wife said
something about her 'Shopping in London and catching a
show' and seeing how the situation was so serious, and
we couldn't get hold of you, I thought it best she send
them here. The only other option being a *'Home'* and
some of them haven't come out of Dicken's days. I don't
think you'd like to think of your precious children
queuing up for gruel" he shot her a strange look and she
hoped she wasn't overacting

"Well I'm sure I can sort out something better than that
til their mother returns. When were they supposed to be
coming?"

Flo looked at her watch "In about ten minutes sir"

"TEN MINUTES?"

She placed a comforting hand on his arm "now don't fret
Mr Parkinson sir, we have everything in hand, Fred's
gone to pick them up from the station and a porter from
the train will escort them to where he's waiting, don't you
worry, he'll get them here safe and sound"

"What he was going to tell Diana , his date for tonight,
was one of the main worries on his mind, he allowed Flo
to lead him out of the office door where she said "Why
don't you have a sit down, I'll bring them straight up to
you as soon as they arrived, we've arranged for them to
be in the room next door to you, and everyone here will
help as much as we can, he walked away in a state of

shock, still not quite believing what he'd heard. He headed to the public phone and rang home, there was no answer. He shook his head and headed upstairs. He'd make the call to cancel Diana when others were out of earshot.

As he disappeared from view Flo said to Alice "so what do you think, was I good?"

"Joan Crawford couldn't have bettered you" replied Alice gleefully. "Every time you called him sir I nearly wet meself, but, I've had a thought, what if the kids tell him it's all a fib? You know what kids are like"

"The kids don't know it's a fib, they think Grandma *is* poorly, sometimes we need to tell little white lies, and they barely saw her anyway, a bit of a jet setter according to Patricia, cards at Easter and birthdays, and the odd visit at Christmas"

The sound of a motor engine told them Fred had returned and he came in a couple of moments later with two handsome looking children, the boy slighter taller than his sister, both the image of their father, who was now walking down the stairs having seen the van arrive from his window. "Daddy" yelled the little girl and ran to him, to be swept up into his arms. For the first time since her arrival, Flo saw something in him she liked. She asked Liz to help them settle in their room and Fred followed behind with her luggage, she'd go and introduce herself properly in a while, but first she had a call to make, to a hotel in London where Patricia was staying til her flight in the morning.and was anxiously waiting to hear that the children had arrived safely.

With Lily's help Flo and Alice prepared the dining room for dinner, laying three place settings at Mr Parkinson's table, the appearance of the children with their still slightly dazed father produced much delighted responses from every one but Miss Tippet and to a lesser degree Alice, she thought the idea of lumbering a philanderer with his kids for a week was inspired but she wasn't over keen at having them around her. To their credit, Jonathan, just turned ten, and Sophie, almost eight, were very well behaved and obviously delighted to be with their father. The kitchen staff rose to the occasion too, and instead of the tapioca served to the grown ups, two huge bowls of jelly and ice cream were placed before their delighted faces.

Flo hovered close to the dining room for the entire sitting. She'd assured Patricia she'd make sure the children were okay and was standing by her word. When her new friend phoned from the south of France, she was confident she'd be able to say everything was fine. She just had to keep her fingers crossed that it had the right outcome. Only time would tell that.

Later that evening, as they sat and watched telly, Alice decided the time had come to tell Flo about the letter. The presence of children on the premises had put her in the happiest mood she'd seen her in for ages

"So what's this you're watching Flo?"

"A comedy with people I've never heard of"

"Is it funny?"

"Have you heard me laughing much?"

"Can't say I have"

"There's your answer. I've smiled a bit but I prefer George Formby"

"I know something that'll give you a laugh"

Flo turned to face her friend, She'd heard something in Alice's voice that told her, she might not find it funny "Go on?"

Alice heard something in the 'go on' "Before I tell you, promise you won't go mad, it was an honest mistake and I'd have told you sooner, but, so much as gone on, what with the Yank and the kids coming -

Flo interjected "Just bloody tell me!"

Alice said nothing, she just pulled an envelope out of her pocket and passed it to Flo

Whats this?

Read the name on the front

"Lucinda Barker? It's for Miss Barker, why have you got

it.? she turned it over and saw the broken seal "and why have you opened it?" There was an undercurrent of anger in her tone, Alice went red and replied "Well, I thought it said Basker and we were told to open their post" Flo scoffed "If it wasn't personal! which this obviously is! and it plainly says Barker, *you* saw the red seal and got nosy! how am I going to explain this?"

"I think you'd better read it, before you say anything else"

"Well, I can tell you have, so I can't see it doing any more harm" She shook her head and muttered to herself *"I don't know HOW I'm going to explain this"* she unfolded the contents of the envelope and began to read

Dear Lucinda

I can imagine this letter will come as a bit of a shock after all these years.

I've known where you are for a while now, but I also know that whilst father was still alive there was no hope of a reconciliation, however as you may know, and if you don't it is with some sadness on my part that I write to tell you of Father's death some twelve months ago.

I wish you could have forgiven him, he was a product of his times and could never have given his permission for you to marry a Blacksmith, But I also understand how cruelly he treated you in this situation, even though I was

*eight years younger, and a mere boy when you left. I
know you never married after parting from Walter ,I have
watched you from afar over the years.And many times I
yearned to contact you. I sadly did not have your bravery
and don't think I'd have made it beyond the walls of
Firsworth and my destiny as Father always put it*

*I am writing dear sister to ask you to come home, if just
for a visit. You have three nephews and a niece you have
never met -I married Alexandra and we eventually learned
to be happy.*

*I am now Lord Firsworth and the gates of Firsworth
house are once again open to the Lord's only sibling Lady
Lucinda Firsworth.*

Please come home Lucy

All my Love, Tarquin

Flo put the letter down "well, that explains the
curtseying" she said dryly

"She's practically royalty" squealed Alice

"I don't know where you get that from"

"How many people do you know whose first name is
Lady? I bet she knows the Queen. They all go to the same
schools, y'know"

"So what if she knows royalty. It doesn't make her any better than us" sniffed Flo, her working class pride kicking in.

"I'm not saying she is" replied Alice "but we know someone not a million miles away who *does* think she's better than everyone else, including Lady Lucy" She gave a triumphant smirk and waited for Flo to cotton on, it didn't take long, she put the letter back into its envelope and placed it in her own pocket "I'll think of a good reason why it's been opened and we'll give it her tomorrow, when she's with her friend" they both chuckled and it was a very relieved Alice that went to bed that night unburdened by the guilt of being a post pilferer.

The next morning, true to her word when persuading Mrs Parkinson to send the children, Flo knocked on David's door before breakfast and announced

"I'm here to help with the children, where are they?" She'd expected them to be up and in daddy's room

"They're still sleeping"

"Still sleeping at this hour!" she exclaimed in mock horror. "I'd best get them up before the day is wasted" To herself she thought '*don't be thinking you can leave them in their room all day'* and without another word she headed next door, gave a quick knock to warn them and she let herself in, they were indeed still sleeping, so she opened the curtains with a flourish and said "Wakey wakey children time to get dressed and have breakfast"

Two sleepy little faces looked back at her and rubbed their eyes, briefly forgetting where they were for a moment, realising this and seeing the tremble in Sophie's lip she smiled and said "Daddy is next door and he's got lots of fun things planned for you" the trembling lip turned immediately into a big smile, and with Flo's help they chose their outfits for the day. A cream shirt with brown shorts and matching pullover for Jonathan and the cutest little summer frock with flowers on it and a pale lemon cardigan for Sophie, she showed Jonathan where the bathroom was and gave Sophie a top and tail in the guest room sink, then, she helped them 'tidy up' before joining their father -it was important to give children chores, and even though Liz and Lily would make the beds proper, she showed them how to straighten the bed sheets and eiderdown, As they tidied, they chatted

"Have you brought any toys with you"

"No" replied Jonathan "I think Mummy forgot, cos Grandma is dying"

Flo gulped "I don't think grandma is dying, yet! so don't fret too much" And then as adults often do she changed the subject without warning, "No toys? Well, I think we need to do something about that, do you know what French Knitting is?" Sophie excitedly said "No, what is it?" Jonathan looked a little crestfallen "Is it a game for girls?" he muttered

"No! It's a game for both girls and boys. Girls can make doilies and hats for their dolls and boys can make" she searched her mind for something boyish "ropes to escape from castle prisons" Jonathan looked intrigued "So how do we French knit?" he enquired

"Well, you go and have breakfast and afterwards I'll teach you. Now scarper off to daddy whilst I get breakfast sorted"

She loved children, she'd have had ten if she could, but, it'd been hard enough having Joyce, She'd lost two before her and two after. In the end her and Bob had decided to settle for what they'd got, although he'd wanted a son he much preferred a healthy wife, pregnancy made her ill. Flo hoped that Joyce would eventually have a dozen or so, for her to love.

While the guests sat down to breakfast, she sought out Fred, gave him two empty cotton reels she'd found in Mrs Basker's sewing basket and asked him to hammer four nails in each. After breakfast she suggested to David that he might want to put his thinking cap on and think of some activities to keep the children amused for the next fortnight, saying, "I'm gonna teach them to French knit, but they won't want to do that all day everyday" It took her half an hour at the most to teach them how to wind the wool around the nails and they were soon engrossed, to the point where she felt 'tight' refusing Mr. Parkinson's request to 'Look after them for a couple of hours whilst he popped into town' She'd already agreed with their mother, that where he went, they went too. He wasn't going to have his cake and eat it. The children were *his* responsibility and he was gonna know it!

"I'm so sorry Mr Parkinson, but it's stock counting day and all the staff have to do it, maybe next time" and with that she swanned off down the corridor, closing the 'staff only' door firmly in his face.

Throughout the day, she also had to deal with Alice pestering her about 'Lady Lucinda' A glance at the to-do book informed her that both Lucy and Miss Tippet would be leaving the guest house that coming Saturday morning for a week in St Anne's, one of their final three considerations as location for the house they planned to buy together, to live out their days after retirement, to shut Alice up, because they had a lot on that week, Flo agreed they'd tackle the situation on Friday, Alice was disappointed but agreeable, she'd waited this long, she could manage a couple more days.

On the Friday evening Flo kept her promise, with a tray containing two cups of cocoa and some custard Creams they made their way to the first floor, "cocoa ladies" said Flo brightly as Miss. Tippet came to the door, she stood aside for them to bring it in, one never did things that servants should do. She often told Lucy off for taking the tray off them at the door. She despaired of Lucy sometimes, she had a common touch about her, would talk to anybody, Abigail's father had dragged him and his family out of a working class life and she had no intentions of ever returning there.

As she carefully placed the tray on a side table, Flo said "there's something else too" she was looking at Miss. Barker, but both women were looking back at her intrigued "Well, spit it out woman" snapped Miss Tippet, Alice could barely contain herself, knowing what was to come, and Flo had to give her a sly dig, "Firstly" she said, eyes firmly fixed on Lucy, I can only apologise for my error" She threw *daggers* at Alice, before turning her attention back to Lucy "I opened a letter addressed to you, in the mistaken belief it was addressed to Mrs Basker"

"Oh don't worry about that" replied Miss Barker, kindly, "It's been done before, remember when I got that invoice for four dozen tea-towels, Abigail? and I was all in a fluster, *that* letter was meant for Mrs basker" She giggled, but her miserable friend just tutted and said "well, pass over the letter then?" both her and Lucy saw the red seal as Flo pulled it out of her Pocket, Miss Tippet was the quicker of the two in grabbing it *secretly aided by Flo who didn't go directly to Lucy with it, and wanted Abigail to get it first,* and her face dropped as she read the contents, with a quick glance to Lucy that said '*This is none of our business*' both her and Alice left the room. Alice stopping briefly to curtsey at the door, before being pushed through it by Flo, outside the door they stood a while, both stifling the urge to laugh at the face on Miss Tippet, as they headed down the stairs to have their own cocoa. Alice quipped "I've seen grass, less green looking than her" Flo responded with, "I've got a green front door less green"

"I know frogs who'd be jealous of her colouring"

"There's not a leaf or a tree outside, as green"

"The world's greenest emerald, isn't as green"

"Robin Hood would kill for cloth that green"

They continued all the way to their quarters and for a good while before going to bed, tomorrow was their last weekend but one in Charge at Oakenelm, Guest House, and it was going to be one to remember.

CHAPTER 20

On Saturday morning, another mystery was solved. completely by accident.

Flo, after checking that Philip's new room was ready for his arrival, and knowing that no one else was residing on that floor, decided to nip to the bathroom because she had forgotten to 'go' when she meant to 'go' earlier on. She'd also forgotten about Sally, and Sally thinking there was no one to share the bathroom with, had not bothered to lock the door, Flo barged in with her legs crossed to be met by a shocked Sally with soap lathered all over her face chest and shoulders, and a razor in her hand.

Both stood in silence just staring at each other before Flo said "*What* are you doing?" her first impression on seeing the razor being Sally was about to kill herself, but the suds confused her.

Sally dropped the razor and burst into tears, Flo's desire to wee disappeared and she found herself sitting on the toilet with the seat down, hugging a heartbroken Sally and getting covered in suds herself, she gave her a few moments to cry it out then started wiping off the soap with a towel, she lifted Sally's face up, with a finger under the chin, "right, tell me what's going on?" she said firmly but kindly "and I give you my word that nothing said in here will leave these four walls"

She was wise enough to know that Sally needed to hear that, before she would confide in her

"I'm a Gorilla" Sally sobbed, and buried her head in Flo's lap again. "Don't be daft" replied Flo "you're dead bonny, I'd kill for eyes like yours and you've such a pretty mouth, when it's not dribbling all over my pinny, now sit up, I don't like talking to back of your head"

Sally sat up,blew her nose with the hanky, Flo offered her, and gave her a weak smile."Thank you, but, you don't understand... I'm too hairy" Flo, being still none the wiser as to why she was so upset said "I could plait my armpit hair sometimes and don't even ask about down there! It's normal luv. All women have it"

"Do *you* have a hairy back and a Mustache?" Cried Sally "because I *do*"

"What do mean a *hairy back*?" and the penny started to drop, for Flo. Aw, bless, is this why you cover yourself from top to toe? And all them mirrors, are they to help you look for hairs? Aw bless, why have you never said anything?" Sally just sobbed some more, whilst Flo rocked her comfortingly. When she seemed a little calmer. Flo turned her face to hers and said "Right, listen to me, nearly every woman I know will shave their 'tache' at some time or another, if they say they don't, they're lying, and as for an hairy back, well, one of me mates an Italian girl had the same problem an' she got some *'oinkment'* off the doctor, now if *you* make an appointment with yours, for next week, I'll go with you if you like?"

Sally, looked at the kind eyes of the older woman sat beside her on the floor "You really know of other people who have this problem?"

"Course I do, You're not *special* " she said, affecting an *uppity* tone, for the first time Sally laughed "That's better" said Flo, "so, are you going to make that appointment?"

"Yes, I am, and I'd like to take you up on your kind offer to go with me"

"It's no trouble at all" said Flo with a smile, to herself, she thought, *I hope she doesn't ask me the name of the oinkment. I've only read about hairy women in TitBits but there is a cream you can get for it -and I didn't tell a complete lie, there was that Italian girl I went to school with who had a bigger 'tache than Kitchener*

"I'd better get a move on" she said, standing up with assistance from Sally "Ooh, me bum's numb, and Alice will think I've been murdered *literally* now, you finish doing what you have to do you, and I'll see you later. Like I said, this goes no further than you and me" Sally's reply was a big hug, "Feeling better?" said Flo "Yes" came the reply, "do you know why that is? 'cos a trouble shared is a trouble halved. Make that appointment, and will you do me one more favour?"

"Of course, if I can"

"When we've been to the doctor's and sorted this out, do you promise to go shopping for some more feminine clothes?" she smiled as she said it and Sally returned her smile as she said "I promise"

Downstairs Alice was hopping about like a woman possessed "where have you *been*?" she hissed, "things to do" replied Flo blithely, this was one secret she wasn't going to share with Alice, the woman had the sensitivity of a brick wall sometimes

"Well, guess what *I've* been doing?"

"Not a lot by the looks of things, why are Fred's tools loitering on the desk, it's not like him to leave things hanging about and he's not even in today, couldn't you have shifted them?"

Alice shot her a dirty look, "Come in the back office" But as she said it the taxi to take Misses Tippet and Barker to the train station arrived. "Hang on a minute" said Flo "I'm not missing this" she called out to Beryl who was just passing and asked her to knock on and tell the ladies their taxi was here, and help them with their bags. Beryl was happy to oblige, she'd thoroughly enjoyed having Flo, and to a much lesser extent, Alice running the guest house.

A few minutes later Beryl came down the stairs bag-less with the two ladies following her. Lucy had always insisted on carrying her own but, Miss Tippet usually insisted a member of staff carry hers, it seemed the events of last night had taught her a valuable lesson. *Class* came from attitude not snobbery. A brief conversation between her and Lucy after breakfast, which Miss Tippet did not attend citing an upset stomach had reassured them both that no damage had been done

"I'll tell you all about it, one day Florence" she had whispered to her new friend

"I think I can read between the lines" Flo had whispered back "Did you love him?"

"With all my heart. Never let anyone tell you who to love"

Thinking of her Bob and the age gap, Flo winked and said "I haven't, and I'll tell you all about that, one day. Will you go and see your brother?"

"I probably will" she smiled

As the ladies headed to the taxi, Abigail with head down, and Lucy looking joyful, she turned to Flo and Alice and said a cheery goodbye, adding to Alice "and stop it with the curtseying, you'll get arthritis in your knees" Flo laughed uproariously and Alice went red. As the taxi drove away. Alice said "Right! back office now. We need to talk" *What now* thought Flo as she wearily followed her to the office. She was relieved to see a pot of tea with steam coming out, on the table. She poured them both a cup and lit a cigarette before saying " Go in then?"

"Well, whilst you were gallivanting about" Flo interjected with an angry tone "I *don't* gallivant, I was working"

"Whatever" said Alice dismissively, anyway, I was doing *proper* work, sorting out the storage cupboard. I don't know who's been in there, but the shelves looked like no one owned them, so I was straightening everything up and guess what?"

Flo knew what was coming, but couldn't be mithered to even ask. Instead she raised a quizzical eyebrow, which Alice took as a response "Him in room three with another tart in his room. I don't know how he's sneaking 'em in, but when staff members go swanning off, what do you expect" she fixed her stare on Flo, waiting for her to look guilty, "I thought we'd sorted all this out?" she replied without a trace of guilt."we had" replied Alice "but only because I let you convince me I hadn't seen what I'd seen when I *had*"

Flo was getting a tad confused and took a sip of tea "so, are you saying that at this moment in time, he has a woman in his room"

"No! But I know when he will have, cos I heard them making plans!"

Flo's interest was aroused, Alice continued "I was just dusting the light fitting before I did the shelves cos I'm not one of those idiots who dusts from bottom to top, and I heard them plain as day, she was asking why she couldn't go shopping and he said we'll discuss it tonight when we get back, plain as day Flo, as God is my witness, I was gonna burst in on them, right there and then, but he could have had a knife or anything" Flo rolled her eyes but Alice was contemplating the thought of being knifed to death, and didn't notice. she shuddered then continued "and then I heard his door open and I just froze. I don't think I breathed for at least ten minutes" Flo did her best not to laugh, as Alice carried on talking "but, then I had a brilliant idea" She waited for the brilliant idea bit to arouse Flo's interest, but she just stared blankly at her. Alice got a bit miffed

"Do you want to hear my plan or *not?*"

"I'm sat here and my ears are with me, aren't they?" she replied dryly, Alice tutted then carried on "well, we don't seem to be able to catch him coming in with them, or leaving with them, but we *can* catch them in the act tonight. And that's why I've got Fred's drill"

"Fred's drill?" asked Flo, her interest piqued, but mainly because she was imagining the damage Alice could do with tools she didn't know how to use "and what do you plan to do with *that?*"

"Drill a hole through the wall from his to the store room" She replied triumphantly

"*Why?*"

"Why? 'cos when we saw them at his bedroom window,

they'd gone by the time we got upstairs, same for when I saw that one's feet under the secret door, and anytime we knock on, only God knows where he hides them but, there's no sign of 'em, this way we can hide in the store room, actually see the woman and just barge in with the master key. Got him bang to rights"

"What if he spots the hole"

"He won't. come with me and I'll show you, it's alright he's gone out and won't be back til later tonight" curious, Flo stood up and followed Alice, who picked up the drill as they passed reception saying "might as well kill two birds with one stone"

A few minutes later, saw them stood in Mr Poole's room staring at the dividing wall

"What do you see Flo"

"Why what do *you* see?" Flo replied with some concern. All she could see was a wall with a couple of pictures and a ship's steering wheel on it"

"See that wheel thing there?"

"Er yes?"

"We're gonna drill a hole through one of them flowers on the wallpaper that show in between the spokes"

"We are? *why?*"

"Cos then we can hide in the store room and catch him in the act" She picked up the drill and advanced to the wall

"Are you sure you know what you're doing with that thing?"

"It's like a whisk, you just turn the handle, Fred showed me, and the wall is the same as they have in them pre-fabs. You know how thin them walls are, we'll be through in seconds"

"I don't know about this. What if we damage the wall?"

"We won't, and if we do, we'll blame him. Look Flo, I know a part of you doesn't believe me, but this is my chance to prove myself right, and get rid of a mass murderer -or at least prove he brings tarts into a respectable establishment, and we've got kids here now" she said slyly, knowing Flo's maternal character

"If we look and see nothing will you give up all this nonsense?"

"Course I will" To herself she thought '*but it's not nonsense*'

Three holes later and a lot of swearing, mainly by Flo, they had a spy hole that gave them a reasonable view of the room, after sweeping up the mess Alice had made and using paper to plug up the unwanted holes, the room looked like no one had been in it. On the other side in the store room, Alice stuck a bit of 'Elastoplast' over the hole, to hide any light should the store room light be turned on, prior to their *stake-out.*, "I don't believe I'm actually agreeing to this madness" muttered Flo as they came back downstairs "Wait and see before you can it madness" said Alice confident of the outcome "oh, by the way this one's got a name, I heard him call her Helen. She'll be praying for Troy to come and rescue her when I've finished"

"Troy's a place not a person"

"Is it? well, you learn something new every day"

Flo wanted to bang her own head on the reception desk "I'm going to see if Philip's arrived. I'll see you later

Philip was in the kitchen having a brew and a catch up with Maureen, as Flo entered he looked up with a smile. "Maureen's just been filling me in about the arrival of the children, well done on two points Flo, the way you dealt with it and the extra revenue" she smiled proudly, "and are you okay with being on the top floor?" she asked "it's just you and Miss Henderson up there this weekend, Doctor Khatta's gone home for a few days" Philip blushed and Flo noticed "erm, of course, in fact I think I'll pop upstairs now and settle in" he paused briefly "are any of the guests in today?"

"Just Miss Henderson" replied Flo trying to sound blase, as soon as he was out of earshot, Maureen said "he fancies her something rotten"

"You don't have to tell *me* that" laughed Flo, "and he may be in for a surprise next week but I'm saying no more, my lips are sealed" It took no more than a brew and a biscuit to unseal them, although, in fairness, no mention was made of the hair problem, Flo just said she managed to convince her to buy some more modern clothes.

After dinner, David and the children bid all a good night and went upstairs for the evening. He had taken them shopping earlier on and they'd come 'home' laden with books and toys *'that's his weekend sorted'* Flo thought with a smile. Mr Poole had already retired to his room, declining dinner as he wasn't hungry and had things to do. *"and we both know what he means by things"* Alice had muttered under her breath, shooting Flo a dirty look when she nudged her hard in the ribs.

Before locking up for the night Alice did a floor check,. Philip was in his room with the door slightly ajar, it annoyed her but she didn't say anything, it *was* his place after all, well, it would *be* one day.

On the second floor she could hear the children giggling as Daddy told them a bedtime story and despite herself, she smiled.

Down on the first floor she double checked Lady Lucinda and her 'common' mate's doors to make sure they were locked and then she went into the store room and stood dead still listening. After a few minutes she heard '*Helen*' It was time for the second operation, she'd given a name. Operation 'Spy hole' .

She didn't rush to find Flo, there was no need, all exits were locked, he couldn't get out of the front door, and it was a steep drop out of the window, even from the first floor, anyway you'd have to be the size of a kid to get through them, no window throughout the house, opened more than a couple of inches, Helen would need to be a midget, with someone to give her a 'leg up' to get through them. The thought crossed her mind '*what if she was a midget?* That would explain how he'd been able to hide her so well. '*she could have been in his bottom drawer and we'd have never known*' She arrived at their rooms "The time has come Flo, he's at it as we speak. I heard 'em in his room" Her tone was cocky

"So, how come you're not jumping up and down like someone demented? I'm amazed you don't want us to put roller skates on so we get there quicker" Flo's tone was sarcastic, she was fed up and feeling very, very homesick. She'd had another postcard off Bob saying nowt, but saying everything...Him and Joyce were alright, but she needed to teach her how to make pastry properly when she came home, cos his heartburn was shocking, and could she explain when she got back why the Club man was still coming, three years after she bought an eiderdown on the weekly.

He'd gone mad when he'd found out she'd got something on tick, his motto was 'Buy it when you can afford it', the

next time she got something, a towel bale, she'd screwed them up a bit and said one of the ladies she cleaned for had given her them. "Must have more money than sense" he'd muttered, they looked brand new, but he'd believed her, the same with the tablecloths and the coat she got for Joyce, more functional than fashionable but beggars and kids couldn't be choosers, she could get fashion when she was making her own money.

She still had her hand on the postcard when Alice had come in thinking she was Elliot Ness, and she'd stared down at it, resting on her lap, as her friend waffled on about windows and midgets. She now stood up, put the postcard in her pinny pocket and said "come on then, let's get this over and done with, we'll give it an hour and if there's no sign of a woman, be she blonde, brunette or bald, we're leaving the store room and *never* mentioning this again. I want to go home Alice, and do normal stuff like watch the telly and argue with our Joyce and make Bob's tea, I'm not cut out for all this nonsense, spying on people - a glass to the wall, or pretending to be tying your shoelace, if they've left the front door open, and they're having a row, is different but, this is like that spy film with that house where they're all Nazis, only these lot are nutters...Except for that American nutter, he *is* a Nazi"

"Bloody 'ell *that* was a speech and a half" exclaimed Alice. She knew Flo, all this would be forgotten in a hour or two, she just needed to let off steam, she was missing her family, Alice understood that but, there was no one for her to miss, and the only person she thought would miss her, was stood next to her, still going on with herself.

"Oh stop moaning" she said, grabbing Flo by the arm and leading her towards the door "we're on the downward slope now, we'll be going home in *days*" she opened the door and after a sigh and a shake of the head, Flo followed her out into the corridor, they were only half way up it, when she felt compelled to ask "Alice, why are you tip toeing?" "do I have to say?" was the whispered reply.

This is going to be the longest hour of my life , thought Flo.

CHAPTER 21

As they quietly climbed the stairs they could hear a distant radio playing Gershwin's *Rhapsody In Blue.*

'I bet that's coming from Philip's room' thought Flo, it was his favourite tune, he'd driven her mad playing it repeatedly on the gramophone, as a child "He's got his soddin' door open" hissed Alice, and then immediately put her finger to her pursed lips and made a shushing noise.

'Bloody hypocrite' thought Flo, and she smiled, she wondered if Philip was hoping to accidentally bump into Sally on the landing. She'd have a word with him tomorrow, he'd be the male version of an 'old maid' if he didn't pull his socks up.

Alice had had the foresight to leave the storage room door unlocked, she'd also realised that if she could hear them, it was highly likely they could hear her and Flo, so, she'd brought some note paper and a pencil, which she mimed having, *badly,* to her companion who rolled her eyes, and sat on an unopened crate of toilet paper, Alice indicated at her to *budge up* and she reluctantly did, thrusting the wrist with her watch on it, into Alice's view and making sure she'd noted the time. one hour she mimed. Who said she *couldn't* play charades?

Alice wrote something down on the paper and passed it over

I think I need the toilet

Flo took the pen, wrote something, and passed the paper back

There's a mop bucket in the corner

Alice gave her the filthiest look she could muster, after another fifteen minutes of mind and bum numbing boredom and just the sound of movement coming from room three, and drawers opening and closing, they heard what they first thought, was music? But, no, it was someone humming in a female voice. Alice gave the best *'I told you so'* face she had ever given, and mimed at Flo to switch the light off whilst she got ready to take the plaster off the wall, Flo did as she was told, the light from the landing affording sufficient light for her to see Alice peering through the hole, and also see the look of absolute triumph as she turned back to her, and indicated that she '*take a look*'

Through the hole she could see part of the bed and the top half of the dressing table, and in slight profile with just her cheeks showing, the head and shoulders of a blonde woman, seated at the edge of the bed, she couldn't see *him* but she heard his voice *"well, what do you think?"* and the woman's voice replying *"I'm just glad to be here"*

'Oh are you?' thought Flo, who was fuming on two levels, one, the blatant flouting of rules, and with children in the house too, and two, how unbearable Alice was going to be now she was proven right, she replaced the plaster and switched the light on. Alice had already begun to write

What are we going to do ????

Flo thought for a minute then started writing *I'll use the master key and we'll just barge in. Let me do the talking!!!*

Alice nodded in agreement, she had no plans to go in first anyway, Flo quietly opened the door and they crept the three of four paces to his door, the thought suddenly struck Flo *'What if his key was in the lock on the other side,* a quick lift of the brass keyhole cover came as a relative relief, the darkness telling her the key hole cover was in place on the other side. With a mimed countdown to Alice of five, four, three and two she held the keyhole cover with one hand, and on *one*, she pushed the key in turned the the lock, then pushed the door wide open.

The woman sat on the bed gasped in surprise, to the left of her on the bed was an opened suitcase. Alice took one look at the contents and screamed *"OH MY GOD HE'S SCALPING THEM!"* and at that point she fainted. Flo didn't even look down, she was transfixed by the woman who had now stood up and was staring back at her and trembling a little. Flo looked to the open suitcase, and looked back at *Helen,* squinting her eyes a little, she said hesitantly,

"Erm, is that *you* Mr. Poole?"

From Helen's mouth came Harold's dejected voice "Yes" and he slumped onto the bed, Flo couldn't think of anything to say but "You should sit up a bit, you'll crease that gown" Harold/Helen looked up in surprise, he hadn't expected such a matter of fact attitude, he was used to the type of reaction he was just about to get from Alice, who, awoken from her faint but still on the floor looked over to the bed, saw the top wig in the suitcase, still assuming it to be a scalp, and started screaming again.

Footsteps from above told Flo that Philip and God knows who else, had been woken by the noise, she had to think and she had to think quick, grabbing Alice by the the shoulder of her pinny, she dragged her out of the door and said loudly "*SHUT UP!*" Just then Philip arrived "what's happened?" he asked looking with concern at Alice still on the floor, do we need an ambulance? or the Police?" the blood curdling scream had convinced him someone was being attacked and he was very perplexed at the sight before him, keeping her hand firmly on Alice's shoulder Flo said

"Do you trust me Philip"

"Implicitly" he replied "but- Flo raised her hand, to his lips in a shushing motion "well, if you do, leave this to me to sort out. no one's injured" she looked down at Alice, who was looking very confused "don't worry about her, this is normal for her, now go to bed and leave everything to me, you tell the other guests that everything is alright. Tell them she saw a spider" Philip looked bemused but had every faith in Flo ,as he turned to go she said "make sure you knock on Miss Henderson's and check she's alright' Philip blushed but agreed, secretly glad for a reason to see her, she hadn't once appeared when he'd *accidentally* left his door ajar.

"What the eck is going on?" said Alice as Philip disappeared from view. "I don't know where to start" replied Flo "but the best way is to show you. Now we're going back in that room, there have been *no* murders, the suitcase was full of wigs, so, have you calmed down? 'cos if you start screaming again, I'm gonna murder your meself"

Alice's only response was 'w*igs?*"

"Yeah, wigs" she paused "how can I put this? Harold wasn't going to murder Helen. Harold *is* Helen.

"Come again?"

"Just be quiet and follow me"

"This time she knocked on room three's door, instead of barging in a *G-Man.* Harold, now almost completely Harold again, but, without the false eyebrows he used to hide Helen's immaculately plucked ones, looked a little odd to say the least; two more suitcase were open on the bed, these were empty ones and he'd started to tip the contents of his drawers in them.

"What are you doing?" asked Flo

"Packing" he replied

"Why?" she asked

"What do you mean *why?*" Interjected Alice "is it not obvious, she turned to Harold "Oy! was that your bloody eye-brow that put the fear of God into me, in the bathroom? you're not bloody normal"

"Alice!" exclaimed Flo, "who bloody is? I'm sorry Harold or should I call you Helen? It dun't bother me, I went to school with a lad who was feminine, got killed in the war but not cos of that, cos of D-Day" She realised she was waffling "look" she said, "it's late, unpack them suitcases and get some sleep, no one's asking you to leave" she elbowed Alice knowing she was about to say something and shot her a warning look. "it's Sunday tomorrow, after breakfast and my chores, I'll come and have a chat with you after. But, let me stress, no one is, *or* will be, asking you to leave, what you do in your private life is your business, and don't mind Alice's face, I don't have to look at her to know she's pulling one" Alice went red and tried to put her face straight. Flo looked at her and said "why don't you go and put the kettle on, and toast some crumpets for me and you. I'll be down in five minutes"

Alice feeling somewhat embarrassed by the whole thing, still couldn't get her head round the thought of Harold Poole, in a *dress!* even if his make up *was* immaculate, and you'd have to proper stare to see it was a man. She was also mortified at the fact she thought wigs were scalps which made her cringe when she thought about it, she was happy, if you could call it that, to oblige Flo's request, and. she left shaking her head.

Of all the possible outcomes, of which, catching him with a midget he kept in the suitcase, was her top choice. Finding out it was him in a frock hadn't even made her top one hundred! wait til she got back home and told people this one, even Valerie Mitchell who'd once gone out with male ballet dancer couldn't top this.

Harold broke the silence first, it wasn't an uncomfortable silence, Flo spent it looking at him in a kindly and slightly inquisitive way

"I can't help who I am, you know? if I could I certainly wouldn't choose living like this, moving from place to place, scared to be found out, because let's have it right. It's *not* normal is it?" The question was meant as a rhetorical one but Flo answered

"It's not normal for a lot of people but it's normal for you. I like cheese with chips, My Bob says *that's* not normal, can I ask you something? she didn't wait for permission "are you more Harold or more Helen?"

He didn't know what it was about this kind faced, middle-ish aged woman but for the first time in a long time, he felt comfortable talking about his secret.

"I was born Harold, but for as long as I can remember
I've felt like Helen, I think my father knew that too, he
accused Mother of making me effeminate, and could
barely look at me, growing up. When I announced I was
leaving home on my twenty-first birthday, his only words
were *'good-bye'* and later Mother wrote to say he had cut
me out of his will and was leaving everything to a distant
nephew, who was in his words a *real man"* Harold closed
his eyes, reliving the moment he read that letter, then
continued his story "I wrote back to say I didn't care for
my father's estate anyway, and only wished to stay in
touch with her, that letter and my next eighteen letters
were returned unopened, and two years later I was told
she had died. When I arrived home" he laughed bitterly
and repeated the word 'home' "the door was shut in my
face, by someone I didn't even know, I stood there for
about fifteen minutes, not daring to knock again, but not
wanting to walk away from my mother's funeral, then *he*
came out of the door and without saying a word, spat in
my face. Two other two men I didn't know escorted me
to the gates and got me a lift...in an ambulance! They beat
me so badly, I didn't wake up for two days, the medics
said I was lucky to be alive."

He took a few moments to compose himself, before
continuing, "It took a long time to regain my memory of
that day, but eventually it all came back. I was physically
sick when I remembered the message they gave to me,
from him, he said I was an abomination and he wished he
could kill me with his bare hands, but, I wasn't worth

getting hanged for! my own father said *that*" He gulped a sob away and took a deep breath "so, I thought if my own father hates me what chance have I with anyone else, and I put Helen away during the day, and was ever conscious of keeping things locked away, I even tried to put her away *forever* and live like a real man, which was stupid because I *felt* like a woman. I lasted two days and realised I couldn't breathe if I couldn't be Helen". He suddenly jerked his head and looked at Flo. "I'm sorry, I'm talking too much"

"I haven't had enough listening yet" smiled Flo "Carry on if you *want* to!"

"That's more or less it. I spend my days and my working life as Harold and my alone time as Helen" He looked quizically at Flo "why are you not shocked? I don't imagine you know many people like me"

"I *was* bloody shocked when I realised it was you in a dress. I'd expected to find you in here but in another part of the room! I've got one of them faces where you can't tell, but believe you me, I was shocked luv. But, eh! once I got used to it being you, I wasn't mithered, you're still you ,whatever your inside leg and girdle size. I've been through the mill meself when it comes to getting called. you should have heard the things people said about me when I when I first married my Bob cos he's a bit older than me"

"By how much?"

"Only thirty years - Gold digger, some of 'em called me. He only had a three bed terrace, God knows what they thought I was digging for! and the other one was, '*his first wife's not even cold yet, in her grave.*' Well, she must have been boiling hot when they put her in her in it, 'cos she'd been dead for six years when we got wed, I know it's not the same as being" she searched for the right word or phrase. "what *do* you call it? Being stuck in the wrong body but with the right brain?

"That's a good enough analogy" said Harold, with a warm shrug of his shoulders and a smile. Flo glanced at her watch. "Gordon Bennett!, look at the time. Alice will be pulling a face when I get back , but, don't mind her, she's daft, but her heart's in the right place, when she puts it in" they both laughed

"I hope to see you at breakfast in the morning?" said Flo, standing up to go.

"I shall be there"

"With your eyebrows?"

His hand shot to his forehead, and he grimaced as he felt his well groomed natural ones "With eyebrows"

She smiled, "You know that I'm going to have to keep calling you Harold whilst I'm here"

"I understand completely"

"But you'll be Helen in me head, I've got enough on my

plate trying to explain all this to Alice, but I know what'll shut her up, God only knows how I'd cope with everyone else" She glanced at her watch for the second time "Right I'm off, definitely this time, I'm shattered, goodnight luv, I hope you sleep well"

"I do believe I will Flo, I do believe I will"

***

She entered the room dying for a brew and ready for a fight with a furious Alice, who she found snoring away on the settee, she grabbed a tartan blanket from the arm of the chair and carefully covered her, then she decided against the risk of waking her with the noise of a boiling kettle and poured herself a cup of the still warmish, *due to the tea cosy,* stewed tea, consoling herself with the fact it was wet, and Alice didn't wake up. With her own eyes heavy, but her brain going nineteen to the dozen she hoped sleep would come soon, she switched off lights and damped down the embers of the fire, before heading to her bedroom, where she tossed and turned for an hour or so, but eventually sleep came.

CHAPTER 22

When Flo woke up on the next morning, Alice was already up and sat at the kitchenette table with a brew and a sour look on her face,

"Five minutes you said"

"And a good morning to you too" said Flo pouring herself a brew and pulling her cigarettes and matches from her dressing gown pocket. "Ooh, it's chilly this morning, and we've still got an hour, I'm gonna switch the 'lectric fire on, and have my brew over there, did you sleep well on that settee?, was it as comfy as mine?"

"Loads comfier actually. yours is springy" she said bitchily, "so what took you so long, were you doing his make up?" she got up from the table and plonked herself down next to Flo.

"Don't be coming out with that kind of rubbish Alice, he can't help who he is"

"Well, what am I supposed to *say*. you don't come across *that* every day, how many men do *we* know, that dress as up as women?"

"How many times? He's *not* dressing up he *is* her"

"Like Olivia De havilland in *Dark Mirror* where she was a good twin and an evil one?"

"No! nothing like that at all! you daft sod. Twins? he's one bloody person!"

"You didn't let me finish. I was *gonna* say, *like* twins but a single version... half man, half woman?" she stared *deadpan* at Flo

"*You're* half woman half idiot. and I haven't got time for this, so, do you want to flush the toilets and help the kids get dressed or do you want to make a start on breakfast?"

Alice didn't need to think long, the thought of getting wriggly kids dressed was far more daunting than bunging sausages in a pan "I'll start on breakfast, but you'll have to come and help me"

"I won't be that long. Right, I'm gonna get dressed and make a start I suggest you do the same"

Her flushing of the toilet on the top floor alerted Philip who been awake about ten minutes, to someone's presence, he popped his head out of the door, and was pleased to see it was Flo "need any help with breakfast?" he asked after wishing her a good morning "no luv, It's all in hand, I tell you what you *can* do though. Could you get the fire going in our room? it's proper nippy today"

"No trouble at all. I'll get one going in the lounge as well. I think Mr Parkinson will be stuck in with the children today. I might wheel the television out for them to watch after Sunday dinner"

"I think that's a wonderful idea luv. I'm getting off now, got toilets to flush and kids to dress, I'll see you later, we need a chat about last night"

On floor two, she flushed the toilet, then popped her head into the children's room to make sure they were awake and instruct them to pick out their outfits but not Sunday best, as they wouldn't be going to church round here, as they did every Sunday with Mummy and very rarely Daddy, neither child was bothered about this change in routine, Sophie sometimes wanted to be a nun, but church was boring.

On floor one, she flushed the toilet than gave a tap on Mr Poole's door, he opened it complete with eyebrows and she smiled "Good morning Mr Poole, And *how* are we this morning?"

"WE are fine he replied, glad for this no nonsense woman, who knew that knocking on the door would break the ice after last night's unconventional chat, he'd sat there for the past hour not daring to even leave his room, even resorting to peeing in his sink, afraid, that as had once happened before, initial amusement would turned to disgust and he and his 'ungodly ways' would be asked to move on,but from the moment he saw her smiling face at the door, he knew there would be no such problem with her.

"I'll see you at breakfast then" and with that she headed back to see how much of a flap Alice was in. she was pleasantly surprise to see her coping, "well done luv" she said approvingly on seeing both the sausages and the bacon already cooked and in their trays "should I do the tea?"

"I've done it, I just need to warm up the tomatoes, and plate up the scrambled eggs and we're ready to go. I'm not completely useless you know. for a woman" and then she added slyly "a *real* woman"

Flo shot her a dirty look "can I just remind you, that Mr. Poole-

"Or Mrs" interjected Alice and started laughing. Flo pursed her lips, then continued "as I was saying *Mr.* Poole is a guest and as a *guest* we respect his privacy2 she fixed Alice with a steely gaze "*one* more joke, and I'll have a joke for the whole of Moston, when we get home. about a woman who fainted at the sight of a wig, now, where's the toast?"

"Oh Bugger! I forgot to do that"

"Never mind, I'll stick it under and bring it through when it's done. You take this lot through"

"I can't push two trolleys on my own" whinged Alice

"Well, take one at a time, then" snapped Flo and started putting slices of bread under the grill.

Alice returned within three minutes, "Philip's in there so, he's sorting out the trays"

"Is everyone down for breakfast"

"They are and you'll be pleased to know that Harold's got his eyebrows on" the warning look from Flo, and the thought of being the subject of gossip in the Post Office queue, made her add "Only joking, I won't say another word" And true to her word, she didn't, mainly because she didn't have time, it seemed like every time she stood still, Flo found something else for her to do, under the guise of "*We're finishing next week, we need to leave the place spick and span so go and have a big clean of the living room and kitchenette, I'll join you as soon as I've bottomed the office, and we'll help each other with the bedrooms*". It all seemed plausible to Alice, She knew Flo's cleaning motto was '*Always leave a place cleaner than you found it*'

As soon as she'd disappeared into the staff quarters, Flo put down her feather duster - the office was immaculate - and collared Philip coming out of the lounge where having positioned the Television near readers corner, he had left the exciting job of tuning it in and getting the aerial in the right position, to Mr Parkinson and two delighted children eager to watch *Childrens Hour,* later that day.

"We need to talk about last night" there was no need for the other staff to know about Mr Poole, yet! but Philip represented the owners and needed to be told, it was her obligation as housekeeper.

An hour later, her and a bemused looking Philip were ready to step out of the office, Philip was still chuckling about Alice thinking the man was a mass murderer and he'd almost fallen off his chair laughing as she recounted the wig incident, at the door he turned to Flo and said "Father has always been of the opinion that what a man does behind the walls of his own home is his business. well, each room here is the guest's home, so as far as I'm concerned what Mr Poole does behind his door is his business" Flo squeezed his arm affectionately. "I'd better go and see how Tilly-bud is getting on, and then make a start on dinner"

"I'll be along shortly to help" he said "I'm just going to show young Jonathan my foolproof design for a paper airplane"

"Boys!" exclaimed Flo in a teasing tone and went to join her friend on the big clean of the Housekeeper's rooms.

After a Sunday dinner of roast beef, potatoes, carrots and Flo's delicious gravy, with trifle for afters and 'ice cream trifle' or the kids, all the guests had gone into the lounge; because it was a Sherry trifle, and Maureen was very generous with the sherry, the children had pulled a face at first, about their dessert, they loved jelly and Ice-cream but had had it three times this week, and wanted trifle, so clever and wise Flo had added a slice of jam roll and sprinkles and told them that theirs was an ice cream trifle, they were delighted and appeased, and wolfed the lot down, feeling sorry for Daddy with his boring ordinary trifle. Daddy, still a tad shell shocked began to recall the events that had brought his children here, as he watched them eat, the *dumping* by Diana earlier in week, who used the most shocking language to him, in their last telephone conversation, had made him understand how unimportant she was to him., the people who loved him in the truest way were these two children eagerly waiting to watch television with him, and if truth be told, Patricia. He felt slightly ashamed and resolved to make it up to her when she got back in a few days. He'd spoken to her once or twice or the phone, she'd seemed in very good spirits considering her mother's ill health and he mentioned this to her, he was relieved for her sake and the children's to hear she'd made an almost miraculous recovery.

When they'd cleared and tidied the dining room, and had eaten their own Sunday dinner, Philip made a little announcement. "you've both worked thoroughly hard these past few weeks and have had to deal with some sticky situations, so I'm giving you both the rest of the day off"

"But what about tea-time?" asked Flo

"All in hand dear Flo" he smiled back "I'm doing it"

"Can you manage?"

"Of course I can., *and* " he smiled shyly "Miss Henderson has offered to help me"

"Ah" said Flo "Right come on Alice, we've got the rest of

271

the day off. it's persisting down so I fancy a bit of telly"

"I fancy a bit of doing sod all" replied Alice, getting up from the table, as they made their way to their rooms Philip called out "I don't want to see either of you this side of the building til tomorrow morning. I'll lock up"

"We don't need telling twice" Alice called back

"Oy cheeky!" said Flo and nudged her friend, but, to be honest she was glad of the break. It *had* been a long and unusual week.

Back in their rooms Flo settled herself in front of the telly and Alice pulled out a book, for a while they sat in silence glued to their respective forms of entertainment, then Alice set down her book and said "This time next week, we'll be home"

"I can't say I won't be pleased. I've loved it here, but I miss normality" replied Flo

"We can't say we have had much of *that* here can we?"

"If you're referring to Mr. Poole" said Flo with eyes narrowing "do you remember what I warned you? you've got enemies on Moston lane, that'd love to have one over on you"

"Bloody ell, stop jumping to conclusions. I wasn't talking about him or her! I was talking in general, to be honest every single one of 'em here is a bit strange, fancy hiding the fact that you're *royal*"

"How many times! she's titled yeah, but that doesn't mean she's royal" Alice ignored her "and her in the attic, hair like a tart, clothes like a nun"

"Will you stop it. She's a lovely girl"

"She's strange in *my* eyes"

"You're strange in *mine!*"

"Then we had a coloured doctor with an English accent"

"And what's strange about that?"

"I didn't realise coloured people could be born here"

"Why ever bloody not"

"Well, don't you have to be born in a hot country to be coloured?"

"If these were my ornaments I'd be throwing one at you now, you don't half come out with some daftness, Alice"

"I've not forgotten the voodoo daftness neither" said Alice, oblivious to her own stupidity

"It wasn't voodoo, he was praying he's one of those Moslems"

"Like Aladdin?"

"I *knew* you'd say summat daft like that, that's why I wasn't gonna tell you til we got home"

"Why ever *not*?"

"'Cos you're an embarrassment Alice, and if I hear one mention of turbans or lamps when you're anywhere near him, I'll lamp you one"

Alice's face said '*no you won't*' and she laughed at Flo's unintentional *'lamp'* joke.

At supper time, Philip knocked on with cocoa and cake and told them he'd decided to stay over an extra night. "any reason?" Flo had asked mischievously "erm, no, no one - I mean, nothing in particular" and he'd hurried out the door.

"I think he fancies her in the attic" said Alice as he left

"You're like Mother Shipton brought back to life, how did you work that one out?" Flo's sarcasm went flying over Alice's head as she replied. "It's a gift I've always had. I can read people, and I'm wise" she searched for the right words, but got lost "I'm one of life's psychopaths like Confucius" Flo didn't even bother correcting her. they both sat in silence for a few minutes, drinking their cocoa before Alice spoke again

"Flo?"

"Yes?"

"This is a serious question now, so please don't think I'm taking the mick. but, when we went in Harold's room last night, I couldn't help but notice his lipstick was lovely, how does she-he-he when he's being she, get his, her lipstick so perfect?" Flo glared at her, but Alice didn't flinch. She *was* being serious "well, will you ask him to show us how to do it?"

"Why don't you ask him yourself"

"*Me?*"

"Yes, *you*"

"*How?*" Flo took deep breaths. It was that or be put on trial for murder! "Knock on his door and say 'Mr. Poole can you show me how you put your lipstick on?"

Alice pulled a face "I might do, if I'm sure I won't catch anything"

"Catch this!" muttered Flo and threw a cushion at her face

"Ow! You could have had me eye out"

"It'll only have gone to that deep dark hole your 'sense' is hiding in, they'll be company for each other, tell me something Alice -and stop being so dramatic, I barely touched you" Alice glared at her, but continued rocking backwards and forwards like she'd been hit by a brick

"No but the cushion you threw did!" she said, sulkily, Flo gave an eye roll "all I want to know, is what you think you could catch from someone like Harold Poole"

"Whatever it is that's he's got!"

Flo felt the *red mist* rising "he's got the desire, the urge, to be a woman! you supposedly already *are one*. I'm going to bed, you're an idiot!"

"Tut! you can't ask a simple question without getting your head ripped off"

"You can if you stop asking questions that are *'simple!* I'm going to bed"

"Make sure you get out on the right side tomorrow, you nowty cow" shouted her friend as Flo slammed her door *extra* hard.

A good nights sleep saw a cheerier Flo, the next morning and a less annoying Alice, it was their last week at Oakenelm and both were looking forward to going home. It looked to be an easy week too, the children's mother had made regular phone calls to check on their welfare and the reports had been food for her soul and her heart, David had risen to the challenge, and the children had loved being with him, he too, seemed to love being with them, not that he had much choice as Flo reminded her with a chuckle filling her in on all her excuses,

"Sorry sir, I've got a pile of napkins to hem"

"I wish I could help but I've got to hold the ladders whilst Alice dusts the dado rails"

Patricia was due back on the following Monday, Flo was

sad she wouldn't get to meet her in person.

She wouldn't get to say goodbye to Lucy and Abigail either, although neither her nor Alice minded if they never saw Abigail again, they'd both taken to Lucy, even if Alice's opinion of her as a 'ditherer' completely changed upon finding out about her 'royal' status. Flo made a mental note to drop her a line, and find out how she got on with her brother, Lord Fauntleroy or whatever it was he was called.

On Thursday, telling Alice she needed to post some letters urgently, she attended a doctor's appointment with Sally, who met her outside the surgery, and where the doctor didn't rush to phone his colleagues because he'd found the first ever case of Gorilla-titus, he merely nodded and reassured her that this was a common problem for some women and prescribed a depilatory cream.

Before setting off for work she hugged Flo and thanked her for her discretion. Flo dismissed her thanks saying "there's no need for all that, just promise me you'll buy a nice frock"

With all the final checks she felt obliged to do before leaving, to ensure everything was spick and span, and no one could call her, the time flew by, and suddenly it was Saturday morning again. Philip had arrived on Friday evening and informed them that all the staff would come in on Sunday and Liz and Lily would be staying over in the empty guest room tonight, because there were no buses early Sunday mornings, and because of that, her and Alice would be relieved of their duties after lunch on Saturday. Flo protested. "As far as I'm concerned I've been paid up to the Sunday, and I don't take money for nowt"

"Well, use the time to give the Housekeeper's rooms a good going over, Philip suggested. "they'll be back on Monday" that *was* acceptable to Flo, they'd clean it top to bottom and mop themselves out when they were ready to leave, by Saturday evening, after a flurry of cleaning, the only thing left to do was to strip the beds when they got up in the morning.

As they enjoyed their special supper, of Welsh rarebit a treat from Liz to say 'thank you' Alice said

"Well, it's certainly been an eye-opener, hasn't it Flo"

"In more ways than one luv"

"People won't believe us when we get back"

"We're not going to tell them everything. *are we*?" said Flo, there was an air of menace in her question, Alice thought about the wigs and cringed "No! no, we're not"

"Right, come on" said Flo getting up from the table "I'll wash, you dry, then I want to watch a bit of telly before bed. It's gonna be murder going back to watching our tiny screen after this massive twenty-four inch one, but I won't miss much else, apart from the people"

"I'll miss the gardens" Alice said folding up the tea towel and draping it over the sink"

"That goes without saying, I bet our backyards look like postage stamps compared to what we've become used to. but still, I wouldn't swap anything for my own life, I've really missed Bob and our Joyce. I can't wait to give them both a kiss and a cuddle. What are you looking forward to most, Alice?"

"Catching that nosy cow Joan rooting round me house. I told her I wouldn't be back til the Monday"

Flo laughed til she cried, already things were getting back to 'normal'

The next morning, they both awoke early, their excitement at going home tinged with a little sadness as they stripped their beds and checked that everything was in order, for Mr and Mrs Basker's return. At ten o clock, they joined the staff for their last breakfast at Oakenelm.

"I'm certainly going to miss all this" said Flo looking with pleasure at the feast that was placed in front of her "we really appreciate you all coming in on a Sunday, if only to say goodbye, don't we Alice?" Alice was chewing a mouthful of bacon, so just nodded in reply,

 "It's been our pleasure" replied Maureen, you've done a cracking job"

"Well, we couldn't have done it without all your help" said Flo, "I'm gonna miss this place, I think I'll have a last look round before we finish off our packing"

"Your taxi's ordered for one o'clock" replied Philip, "Why don't you come through to reception at about half past twelve and have a final look round then? I know *you* Flo, you'll start tidying up things,if you have a walk round now, so skedaddle! you'll have more than enough to catch up on when you get home, sit down and relax for a bit, with the Sunday papers" he thrust copies of that morning's *Sunday Post* and *News Of The World* in her hands as he said it "Well, if you insist" she replied with a smile "come on Alice, let's go and be ladies of leisure for an hour.

Back in their rooms, with a fresh pot of tea, and a Woodbine for Flo, they sat in blissful silence, catching up on scandals, and 'Oor Willie' comic strip adventures. At just after twelve, they made their final checks of the room and put their coats on, before heading for reception. "I'm glad we said our goodbyes earlier on" said Flo, as they walked past the empty kitchen, they must all be busy, we might catch them in the dining room though"

"Why?" replied Alice "how many times do you need to say 'bye' to someone?" Flo tutted "You're such a people person aren't you?"

"Can't stand most of them, if I'm honest" replied Alice, Flo's sarcasm going right over her head.

Reception was 'empty' too, but they could see Philip pottering about in the back office, Alice 'dinged' the bell and responded to Flo's 'dirty' look, with a look of her own that said '*I don't work here anymore, I can 'ding' what I like*'

"Hello ladies" said Philip, coming out from the office "Is it that time already? We've been run off our feet here"

"You should have said" replied Flo a little miffed "we've been sat on our backsides doing nowt all morning"

'*Speak for yourself* 'thought Alice. Philip just grinned before saying "Come on then, you can say 'goodbye' to the lounge and dining room first, and then we'll have a wander upstairs" he led the way into the lounge, and it was a good few minutes before either woman could speak.

Stood before them, was not only every single guest, but, all the staff members, and Doctor and Mrs Howarth too, they all burst into a chorus of '*For they are jolly good fellows*' whilst Flo burst into tears and Alice looked slightly mortified.

"You bloody swines" spluttered Flo through her 'happy' tears, addressing the whole room as Philip guided her and Alice toward a couple of dining chairs placed incongruously in the middle of the room, and instructed them to sit down.

One by one, the guests came forward, the children first, "thank you for looking after us" said a shy sounding

Jonathan "and thank you for teaching us how to 'French knit' we've made you this" and he thrust something she assumed to be a doily in her hand, adding "Mrs Clough showed us how to sew it up but she said she didn't want one, so we've just made one for you"

"Really?" replied Flo, looking at Alice with a smile, she'd be getting teased when they got back home.

'I thought you didn't like kids? and there you were teaching them to sew behind my back"

She found herself being almost suffocated by their squeezes, and then their Father came forward to add his good wishes. He was accompanied by a woman Flo didn't recognise, til the 'penny' dropped

"Patricia? Is that *you"* she exclaimed in surprise "I thought you weren't due back until tomorrow?"

"I lied" came the reply and she leaned over to give Flo a hug and whispered "thank you" before giving a hug of thanks to Alice, she was followed by Miss Tippet and 'Lady' Lucy, a handshake and curt thank you from Abigail, who at least had the grace to look 'humble' and a big squeeze for both of them from Lucy, after the ladies, they found themselves receiving 'thank you's' and hugs from Doctor khatta and Harold Poole, who both ladies were slightly relieved to see, had his eyebrows on. Alice stiffened a little at *his* embrace, no matter what Flo said, he was *not* normal.

They then found themselves staring at another 'stranger' until once again, the penny dropped, the beautiful young woman in the 'Dior' type dress, stood before them, was Sally "Oh my goodness" exclaimed Flo "you look beautiful Sally, come here and give me a hug" as they embraced she whispered "well done luv, well done" and she looked over at Philip and gave him a wink, which he returned with a reddening face, all Alice could think was *'talk about one extreme to the other, you can almost see her bosoms in that dress.'*

Their final 'thanks' came from Doctor and Mrs Haworth, who joked about Philip's 'slyness' in arranging all this, and disappeared into the back office with Flo for a few minutes. *'probably to pay her'* mused Alice not really mithered because she was basking in her own glow of thank yous from the residents, when Flo and the guest house owners reappeared, they all had big smiles on their faces *'she must have got a bonus'* thought Alice, before exclaiming "Flo, the time!" Philip made the reply for her,

"Another little white lie, I'm afraid, there's no taxi ordered yet, because we need to give you this" On cue, Maureen appeared with a trolley, holding the most beautiful cake they'd ever seen; white icing covered the square cake, and delicate purple iced flowers were dotted all over it. Alice whispered in Flo's ear *'isn't purple for 'death'?*' and received a nip to the arm for her trouble, whilst everyone sang another chorus of *for they are jolly good fellows*

With the cake cut up and shared out, the leftover piece wrapped in wax paper for Flo and Alice to take home, a voice shouted "Speech!" and all eyes were on Flo, who for the first time in her life, looked shy, but she stood up, cleared her throat and said "I'm overwhelmed -we're overwhelmed" she said, looking at Alice who grinned, mainly at her friend's discomfort, before continuing "I've never even had a Birthday party, but I have had a grand time working here, and beyond that I don't know what else to say, other than thank you, and it's been a pleasure to meet every single one of you, hasn't it Alice" Alice hesitated for a moment and said "Yeah" in a not very convincing manner, she was still 'iffy' about Harold/Helen and was ready to go home now, because she had a feeling she was gonna catch Joan in a compromising situation, rooting through her stuff.

Finally the taxi did arrive and it was time to go, several more hugs, an invitation for Patricia *to come for tea one afternoon, and meet Bob* and promises to keep in touch with staff *and* guests, delayed them a few minutes more, but, they soon found themselves sat in the back of a black cab "Where to ladies?" asked the driver and he climbed into his cab and began driving out of the grounds.

"Moston lane, luv" replied Flo, turning to wave at at people who become friends, and people who had become family, who had all gathered outside the guest house, to wave them off "We're going home"

EPILOGUE

The twin tub was delivered a week after she'd arrived home, to a big hug from Bob, and a blase "hello Mother" from Joyce, although, she didn't shrink away when Flo hugged *her*. The next few days after its arrival were spent washing anything that moved, including Bob's good suit, which shrank in Flo's favoured 'boil wash'

'It's a good job I've got a few quid leftover' she thought *'He's gonna need that suit, someone he knows is bound to die sooner or later, but I won't mention what's happened til I need to'*

It took another week or two for her to get the house back to *her* standard *"There's more to cleaning a cooker, than cleaning the cooker!"* she'd shouted at a bemused Joyce *"there's enough grease on the wall behind it, to fry chips in!"*

As she scrubbed the house from top to bottom she was glad of the break from Alice, who had used her 'wages' to fund a visit to her cousin Murial in Scarborough, where Flo just knew she be regaling anyone who would listen, with exaggerated accounts of her involvement in the lives of the guests,

"So I said to Flo, you need to get his wife and kids down here, and you need to do it quick"

I knew from the start it was a man in a dress, no woman I know has hips that slim"

"It's not the done thing to talk about one's 'royal connections, but, believe you me, I've got 'em"

"It was my war-time training - I was gonna be sent to France as a spy, but the war went and ended -that first made me suspect, the American was a Nazi"

She was relieved when finally, the house was as clean as could be, especially as they were expecting a guest to 'Tea' that afternoon, she hoped Bob hadn't forgot to get the ham for butties, *"he's cutting it fine"* she said to herself looking at the clock on the mantle-piece, but the sound of him coming up the lobby made her relax a little "you've haven't forgotten we've got someone coming for tea have you?" she asked, helping him off with his coat, "If I had" he replied grumpily, this daft collar would be sitting on the sideboard by now, Flo shook her head, straightened his tie and kissed him on the forehead before heading to the scullery to make sandwiches and put slices of Battenburg and Madeira onto her poshest tiered cake stand,

At a quarter to three, there was a knock on the front door, and Flo shouted "I'll get it" as she came hurrying out of the scullery, wiping imaginary dust off the door frame as she passed, and giving Bob a last minute check before pulling her pinny off, and heading to the front door. As he heard squealed greetings, and footsteps coming closer, he stood up to greet their guest, hoping she didn't have a gob like Alice, because, he couldn't face the thought of an hour or two listen to two clucking hens. He also hoped she'd be gone before the Pools results came on.

Introductions were made, small talk indulged in, and a fine spread was served up by Flo, after having their fill, tea was served on the coffee table opposite and Bob was able to escape to his chair and newspaper, no more being required of him than confirmation of whatever it was she was going on about

"So I told her, didn't I Bob? Just 'cos I've got a twin-tub it doesn't mean I'm a Launderette, I mean, who in their right mind, pops round to someone's house, for a brew, with a bag of dirty sheets?"

"You're not wrong luv"

It had turned out to be a very pleasant afternoon, Flo's friend was well spoken, well, dressed well mannered and entertaining company, she was quite attractive too, but, that didn't matter anyway, Bob was strictly a one woman, man, no woman he met was *ever* a patch on his Flo. He sat with his paper and pipe, occasionally smiling as he listened to Flo and her friend chat and reminisce, and smiled some more, when her charming friend stood up to leave, a good fifteen minutes before the results were read out. Bob, as he always did, stood up as goodbyes were said, and then Flo, accompanied her friend to the door. As usual, she took 'ages', and Bob was sat at the table, crumpled up pools coupon in hand when she returned.

"So, what do you think of her?" she said, clearing away the remaining pots "seems like a nice woman" he said before adding bluntly, "better than some friends you have" Flo grinned, and he continued "speaking of Alice, have you told her that you're both going to be special guests at the guest house?"

"Not yet" she smiled, "It's not til after next Easter anyway, there'll be no shutting her up if she knows we're going back, and if she finds out there's going to be a wedding, we'll have to relive her and Eddies all over again and visit Kendals every soddin week for 'ideas'" she paused visualising what would happen if Alice knew, and she shuddered "no luv, I'm keeping my mouth shut"

"I wish she'd keep *hers* shut" Bob replied she could shatter glass when she's 'on one' you should get your friend to give her elocution lessons"

"Good idea" said Flo with a smile, Bob continued "what's her name again? I can't keep calling her your friend"

"It's Helen, luv... Helen Poole"

ABOUT THE AUTHOR

The author was born in Manchester 1960 to a Barbadian father and English mother, the first of their six children, and is proud to be a Mancunian with a *twist*

This is her third book, and first Novel, her previous books being a collection of stories based on her life growing up in 60s/70s Manchester as part of a multicultural family, and the characters she was either related to or came into contact with.

She currently resides in Bolton which she regards as *abroad* and is a proud mum and extremely boastful nana.

She hopes her writing makes people laugh, and on a serious note, she hopes it highlights the absurdities of bigotry and prejudice

Should anyone except the Club man wish to get in touch, she can be contacted by email: aminaa1@btinternet.com Or via her Facebook page: A. L Mottley